SIX FOR SAINT-PIERRE

Kevin Major

The author is immensely grateful to the people of Saint-Pierre who were so generous in answering research questions, including at le Francoforum *and* la Gendarmerie nationale. *He extends his heartfelt appreciation to editor Marnie Parsons and the team at Breakwater Books for their commitment and guidance.* Un grand merci à tous!

For its support, the author wishes to thank ArtsNL, which last year invested $2.24 million to foster and promote the creation and enjoyment of the arts for the benefit of all Newfoundlanders and Labradorians.

BREAKWATER BOOKS LIMITED
P.O. Box 2188, St. John's, NL Canada A1C 6E6
WWW.BREAKWATERBOOKS.COM

LIBRARY AND ARCHIVES CANADA CATALOGUING IN PUBLICATION
Six for Saint-Pierre / by Kevin Major.
Major, Kevin, author
Canadiana (print) 20250175096 | Canadiana (ebook) 2025017510X
ISBN 9781778530654 (softcover) | ISBN 9781778530661 (EPUB)
LCGFT: Detective and mystery fiction. | LCGFT: Novels.
LCC PS8576.A523 S59 2025 | DDC C813/.54—dc23

COVER IMAGE: Photo of Saint-Pierre by Kevin Major; storm clouds by John D Sirlin, Shutterstock; compilation by Beth Oberholtzer, Oberholtzer Design Inc.

PAGE LAYOUT: Nadine Hodder

THE PUBLISHER GRATEFULLY ACKNOWLEDGES THE SUPPORT OF the Canada Council for the Arts, the Government of Canada through the Department of Heritage, and the Government of Newfoundland and Labrador through the Department of Tourism, Culture, Arts and Recreation.

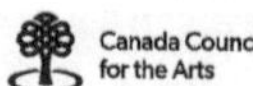

Newfoundland Labrador

PRINTED AND BOUND IN CANADA.

Breakwater Books is commited to choosing papers and materials for our books that help to protect our environment. This book is printed on paper made of material from well-managed forests.

Vive Saint-Pierre-et-Miquelon, des voisins extraordinaires.

The body, cast against shoreline rocks in a remote part of the island, lay entrenched in coarse sand and seaweed, cold surf lapping over them. Bare except for swim shorts, brightly coloured and patterned with sea creatures—a morbid contrast to the pallid flesh.

Had he been disorientated by the sea temperature, the young man could well have fallen and struck his head against one of the rocks and drowned, or so the perpetrator must have hoped the police would conclude. La Gendarmerie nationale *discovered a lesion to the victim's skull, but a wound to his right thigh told a different story.*

A story of abandonment that, as it turned out, unfolded on Île aux Marins, an island that was itself abandoned decades before.

Resettled, deserted communities are part of the history of Newfoundland, and so too of Saint-Pierre and Miquelon off Newfoundland's south coast, an overseas territory of France.

Yes, France. A curious remnant of the Anglo-French Wars of centuries past, with a population, concentrated in its capital, itself called Saint-Pierre, of a mere six thousand souls.

In its harbour is the island, once a thriving community, now a haven for nostalgic locals and a destination for tourists.

One visitor fit neither category.

That person arrived on Île aux Marins with no leisurely intent whatsoever.

ONE

LIFE IS A highway, all signs pointing to exhilarating days ahead.

With Mae Lainey, my one and only. Keyed up. All systems go.

A stellar final tour for the season over and done with. Gaffer the dog comfortably at the home of my ex-wife and her partner, at her suggestion no less. St. John's now far behind, Mae sitting contentedly in the passenger seat, reminiscing about our first road trip together.

'I have the feeling this one will be even better.' Her smile meets my own. 'No discovery of a dead body within hours of checking into the guesthouse.'

I remember it only too well. It put a rather heavy damper on a much-anticipated romantic interlude. Let's not go there.

'Ah, Morris the famous Moose.' If there's a landmark in my highway travel it's the life-size statue at Goobies, just before the turnoff to route 210. 'Gaffer's favourite.' Whenever the dog had occasion to stop here, he took particular pleasure in raising a hind leg to the ungulate's hoof.

This time we bypass Morris in favour of a pit stop for coffee and a couple of pre-made breakfast sandwiches. No better accompaniment to heading down the Burin Peninsula than that still warm combo of egg, bacon, and cheese on a toasted

English muffin. When all is said and done, I'm a man of simple pleasures. Over the next week we're on course for several more, highlighted by a jaunt across the water to Saint-Pierre and Miquelon.

First up is an encounter with Rencontre East.

Despite half the name, it's not French. Nor for that matter is Bay L'Argent, a hundred kilometres down the peninsula, the community where we catch the ferry that will take us there. (The French *were* here, but these places ended up on the losing side of the Anglo-French Wars.)

No matter, we're not here for the foie gras, but for the singular pleasure of being in a place where there's no practical way in or out except by boat.

The ferry turns into an inlet of Fortune Bay and strikes Rencontre East, brilliant in the September sunshine. High rounded hills covered with stunted evergreens are the backdrop to its scattering of homes. They've been built on a gently sloped shelf of land that eventually drops away to a shoreline marked by wharves and fishing sheds.

As the ferry ties up we're on deck surveying an outport of 115 residents, and a welcome sign that confirms Rencontre East is "isolated and loving it."

Not a car or truck in sight. Not a stop sign, not a traffic light. No cops, no smog, no Walmart. What more could you ask for?

As it turns out, not a heck of a lot. Forward-thinking Mae has packed a thermos of coffee and picnic provisions, so we're off to explore for the next few hours, until the return run of the ferry to Bay L'Argent.

First—Judy's General Store. A general store is my go-to stop when in need of insight into an outport's points of interest. And an ice cream bar my go-to purchase, a small gesture of support for the business. Mae hovers nearby in search of something healthier.

The clerk is super helpful in providing directions to the Downton's Pond Trail. 'It's not long, and once you get there it's gorgeous. You'll love it.'

'How about elevation gain?'

She smiles. I suspect I came off sounding like a townie.

'It has its ups and downs,' she says, handing back my change. 'But no need to waste your money on an energy drink.'

Outport wit—I love it. You talk to a stranger for less than a minute and she has you laughing. Sweet.

She checks in Mae's small stockpile of fruit and granola bars, with an aside to me. 'If it's elevation you're after, try the lookout. Uphill all the way.'

We're off then, smiling still.

With its scattering of fall colours, the hike circling the pond is a feast in itself, and proves especially restorative. We hold hands all the way. Untamed nature is such a powerful force for good.

Unfortunately, we're soon back at our starting point. It's not a big pond and, we both agree, not one to build up much of an appetite.

'How about a jaunt to the lookout? We've got plenty of time.'

'Just what the doctor ordered.' That would be Doctor Frank, my no-nonsense GP who a few years back led me on the path to shedding twenty pounds. (He threatened me with diabetes.)

Rigid adherence to my regime of choice, Intermittent Fasting, did the trick and here I am shipshape and ready to tackle the incline. Elevation gain yet to be determined.

But more than expected. As promised, uphill all the way. By the time we reach the lookout I'm breathless.

Aptly—the view is breathtaking. 'Absolutely worth it,' I manage on the exhale. Such a spectacular view of the outport, its harbour, and the open ocean beyond. Rencontre East might be isolated, but you can't help but love it.

Bring on the food. Let's get back to breathing normally and boost the panorama with spicy egg sandwiches, olives, and pickled onions. And the priceless contribution from Judy's General Store.

While I dip a granola bar in a mug of still hot coffee, it seems a good time to check in with son Nick to let him know we're on our way. We'll see him in a couple of days.

After his first year of university at King's College in Halifax, Nick came back to St. John's and continued his arts degree at MUN, majoring in English, with a minor in French. His second year back has brought him to Saint-Pierre, where the university has a language institute. Students spend a semester in total immersion.

Such is the advantage of living next door to a piece of France. There's every indication he's thoroughly enjoying it. I gather he's acquired a taste for French wines. Among other things I'm sure, with him soon to turn twenty, *la testostérone* at its peak.

'Hey, Nick, how's it goin'?'

'Great. Excellent as a matter of fact. Looking forward to seeing you guys.'

Which is a relief. I'd been thinking that after three weeks of living life on his own terms, no parent in sight, his father's arrival might not go over particularly well.

On the contrary. 'I thought when you get here we could all go out to dinner.'

'For sure.' Of course, one of the upsides of me showing up is getting to eat out on dad's dime.

'There's some excellent restaurants here. I've done some research.'

I'm sure he has. Over the years the lad has developed a fondness for restaurants, usually ones well beyond his budget. When he lives with me we cook together day in, day out, the more adventuresome the better, which I would have thought was enough to quell his craving for restaurant food. Not the case. In fact, spending summers employed as a waiter has upped his enthusiasm for places with more inventive (i.e., pricier) menus than where he's worked.

He's perfected the habit of building a list of what he calls "potentials." Meaning he can't afford them, but maybe his father or mother can, if only on special occasions. Such as this one—reunion with a parent after three whole weeks.

We keep the call short. The island of Saint-Pierre is all of twenty kilometres from Newfoundland, but Bell Canada is only too happy to slap on international calling rates.

Nick's agreed to meet us at the dock when we arrive on Sunday, about five-thirty, just in time to check into our accommodation and head for one of Saint-Pierre's finest dining establishments. My credit card is already bracing for the hit.

Jesting aside, it will be great to see him, to see how he's faring on foreign soil. As part of his course requirements he's expected to speak only French, although he'll have to make an exception for his language-deficient dad. And for Mae, who, although somewhat more proficient than I am, has her limitations.

It's back to the scenario at hand. We soak up a bit more of the view before reversing the elevation gain and making our way to the dock. We arrive a little early, with the expectation that it's a gathering place for local folks with time on their hands. An opportunity to chat and come away with a better sense of the place. Something I'm always keen to do when I travel.

It's obvious we're tourists. 'Enjoyed the lookout?' I'm asked. In a place this size, nothing goes unnoticed. The man walks closer to us with the help of his cane. 'Fine view from up there.'

'Absolutely.'

We're joined by a young lad, maybe twelve, a fishing rod in his hand. And wearing what elicits a double take on my part—a jazzy, floral-print running cap. Ultralight and very trendy.

'Where you from?' he asks, bold but easygoing.

'St. John's.'

I detect disappointment. 'We sees 'em from all over the place, don't we, Uncle Joe. A fellow here a few days ago from Martinique.'

'Martinique is right, Liam.'

In both cases the pronunciation is off but I take it to be the island in the Caribbean. 'Really?'

'Hes English wasn't the best, but we had a fine chat all the same,' says Joe, who's likely Liam's great-uncle. Or not, it being rural Newfoundland where it's common for anyone getting on in years to be called aunt or uncle, even if they're no relation.

'On his way to Saint-Pierre, I expect?' Given that Martinique, if I recall correctly, is also an overseas territory of France.

'Yes, no surprise there,' says Joe. 'Not many tourists shows up in Rencontre without they was in Saint-Pierre or are heading there.'

What *is* a surprise, to me at least, is that someone from a small island in the West Indies would show up at all, let alone this time of the year.

'He give me this,' says Liam, pointing to his cap. 'Hes name is on the label.'

I look at Mae, who I assume is thinking what I'm thinking—rather an odd thing for a stranger to be doing, even if he did design the cap himself.

Liam sinks a hand in the back pocket of his jeans and fishes out a card. He hands it to Mae.

A business card. She studies it, then passes it to me.

Philippe Jean. Couturier. Casual with Class. Les Trois-Îlets, Martinique.

Words embossed over the scene of a palm tree leaning toward the turquoise waters of a pristine sandy beach. I return it to Liam.

He takes out his phone and begins scrolling. He stops, scrolls back one screen and delivers the phone to me. It's Liam in the running cap, standing next to a young black man of medium height with a head of short, spiky, bleach-tipped curls. He's wearing a thin, lime green puffer jacket, skin-tight jeans, multicoloured sneakers, and blue-tinted, wraparound sunglasses. Looking rather incongruous in outport Newfoundland.

I now see why a middle-aged couple from St. John's sporting charcoal Columbia fleece and nondescript hiking boots would get mixed reviews.

We board the ferry, having ended our afternoon in Rencontre East on a memorable note. There was a time when a visit to a Newfoundland outport would leave you with the feeling that the glare of the broader world had passed it by. That you had stepped into an innocent, changeless scene. No more. What Mae and I are now leaving behind is a lad fishing off the side of the dock, Caribbean running hat on his head, rod in his right hand, phone in his left, all the while madly texting with one thumb. He takes a second to raise his phone hand and wave goodbye.

Joe, at least, is holding nothing but his cane. That's reassuring. We wave back eagerly.

In less than two hours we're docked back in Bay L'Argent, and on our way to our accommodation for the night. We drive further south on the 210, down "The Boot," as the peninsula is affectionately called, due to the fact its lower end where its towns are concentrated is shaped like a well-clad foot. We make a brief stop at a supermarket in Marystown, at the ankle of the peninsula, before turning off to reach the upper end of the instep and a place called Garnish.

The place name alone was enough to pique my interest when we were making plans for the trip. As Mae would say, I have this thing about Newfoundland place names. While Garnish doesn't have the carnal qualities of a Dildo or Leading Tickles, nor the corporeal connotation of, say, Joe Batt's Arm or Jerry's Nose, there is a certain innate allure to the name, especially to lovers of a well-prepared meal, such as ourselves. While many would say the origin of the name is unknown, I like to think it must have had something to do with the abundance of cod, herring, salmon, lobster, etc., etc., and the keen cooks aboard the first fishing vessels to arrive here.

The A-frame cottage overlooking Fortune Bay was somewhat secondary in choosing Garnish, although we are more than charmed by its knotty pine interior and the handmade quilt on the queen-size bed. Let's just say the rustic flavour creates a certain untamed atmosphere. Setting the scene for this, the first evening of our getaway.

We managed to secure some Fortune Bay scallops in Marystown. Over time I've fine-tuned a recipe for scallops. Pan-seared in white wine, balsamic vinegar, and Dijon. Over a bed of lemon pasta and cherry tomatoes. Garnished with fresh tarragon.

'Amazing,' says Mae. Leaving me chuffed.

Post-dinner we bundle up and sit on the deck overlooking the moonlit bay, finishing off the Chenin Blanc Mae chose, the perfect match for the scallops. And a perfect match for winding down on a day that saw us go from urban hustle to the wiles of rural seclusion. A more sensual garnish to the day has yet to be revealed.

For a man whose internal clock is programmed to have him up and on the go by seven each morning, there is something wonderfully decadent about lying curled against your partner with the LED glow from the night table reading 8:27, and counting.

Mae is the one to finally make the move. She shifts my arm from around her and advances to the side of the bed.

'Ahhh.' That would be me, giving voice to my disappointment at the thought there's a world beyond the bedcovers.

'I'll fry some bacon,' calls Mae.

If there's a lure that draws my naked self out of its comfort zone, it's the smell of bacon frying. Especially the double smoked, dry cured, thick cut variety I saw Mae place in the cooler when we were packing for the trip. Over the time we have been together she has noted my weaknesses and learned to play them to her advantage.

Even so, I'm careful to restrict the intake of fat-laden, processed food. Then again, hey, we're on holiday. I cast aside any second thoughts about living in dietary sin.

Bacon and free-range eggs, toast with Seville orange marmalade, freshly ground coffee doing its thing in my AeroPress. As I said, a man of simple (if precisely chosen) pleasures. Perfect accompaniment to an unhurried, easygoing start to the morning.

It is eleven before we've checked out and are back on the road. We backtrack slightly, bypassing Marystown and a second sizable town, Burin, heading to the heel of the peninsula, and the community of St. Lawrence.

We're here to pick up the walking trail to Chambers Cove. We've chosen it for a very good reason.

There are many remarkable stories of survival along the coasts of Newfoundland and Labrador, but few to surpass what happened up and down the cliffs of Chambers Cove in the dead of winter, 1942.

'I feel we're approaching sacred ground,' says Mae, as we near the cliffs and come in sight of the reefs on which the USS *Truxtun* had wrecked. It was one of two US Navy ships to run aground and break apart in a blinding storm one February night.

One hundred and ten men of the *Truxtun* were lost, but against all odds, forty-six survived, with the help of men from St. Lawrence who navigated the icy cliffs to reach those who made it to shore alive. The sailors, some barefoot, most thinly clad and covered in oil, were led up the cliffs and into the homes of St. Lawrence where the women of the community cleaned and cared for them, revived them after the horrors of their ordeal.

Mae and I recall the story of one man in particular, whose personal experience transcended survival. His name was Lanier Phillips, eighteen years old at the time, an African American raised in segregated Georgia. His astonishment at being so lovingly cared for by the white inhabitants of St. Lawrence empowered him to confront the discrimination that had been his daily life. He marched with Martin Luther King Jr. and fought to become the Navy's first black sonar technician. His story flashes before me as I peer over the cliff to the narrow beach below—the horrific struggle of the young man in the frigid, wind-battered, oil-choked waters of Chambers Cove.

'From time to time we all complain about what life throws at us. We should thank our lucky stars.'

The continuation of our drive along the arch of the peninsula brings us to Lawn, which has its own story to tell, of how eight men walked ten miles to reach survivors from the wreck of the USS *Pollux*, the other ship to run aground that night, hauling them by rope, one man at a time, up and over the face of the cliff. Of the two hundred and thirty-three men aboard the ship, one hundred and forty survived.

A sobering thought as we drive toward Lord's Cove, the next community along our route, and one that's had its own share of disaster, which we hold off mentioning for the time being. We need a respite, a break from the historical to something more immediate.

'A swim anyone?' says Mae.

Not my first line of thought. A sunny day, but it's fall in Newfoundland nonetheless.

Mae has led us to Sandy Cove, a beach just outside Lord's Cove. 'A hidden gem of the Burin Peninsula,' as she quotes from the tourist brochure. It is that—a broad expanse of fine, reddish sand quietly lapped by the North Atlantic. Beautiful. Very impressive. But let's be clear, the water is bound to be frigid. As confirmed by the fact that the beach is completely deserted.

'On average, about 10°C,' she informs me. She's done additional research while the bacon was frying, apparently.

'Guaranteed hypothermia.'

'Really, Sebastian. Afraid your gonads will shrivel?'

Mae has a way with words. I'm smiling, stiffly.

'My "gonads," as you lovingly refer to them, are quite capable of maintaining their standard size. Not that I have any intention of testing the theory. I'm willing to kick about the water in my bare feet, but that's the extent of it.'

She says nothing. Instead, she begins to remove her clothing. Down to what is revealed to be a one-piece swimsuit that I can only assume she donned in the interval between her beach research and the bacon having concluded its time in the fry pan.

'Really?' She looks very good in the swimsuit, her summer tan still in evidence. That, however, is decidedly beside the point.

She places her discarded clothes inside a tote and moves it to safety above the waterline, all the while continuing her silence. She smiles cheekily as she passes me at the water's edge, where I stand barefoot, jeans rolled above my ankles.

Let's just see how far she gets before doing an abrupt U-turn and racing back to shore. I can't wait.

Surprisingly, I do wait, and continue to do so. She walks steadily, without flinching (with supreme effort, undoubtedly). As far as her knees, then her thighs, to the firm (and getting firmer) buttocks. At which point she springs forward and dives into the water. She emerges, the water chest high, looking in my direction.

My gonads urge me to action. The man in me is chagrined. 'I don't have any trunks?' I call out.

Resoundingly lame.

Mae dives a second time.

Little time passes before I stand naked, bar my boxer briefs.

If I'm going to redeem myself I have but one choice. Boxers off, I hop to regain my balance, then race straight into the water, ignoring as much as is humanly possible the ice water that attacks my flesh. Sweet Jesus.

I am, against all odds, grinning when I reach Mae, arms outstretched. We embrace, laughing outrageously.

As soon as we detach, she runs toward shore. I'm tight behind her. She goes straight for her tote, removing a pair of towels, tossing one to me. Clearly, all had unfolded as planned.

I don't complain. I'm too busy drying the gooseflesh, manoeuvring the too-small towel so that part of it covers the shrunken gonadal area.

Suddenly, in the near distance comes the sound of a motorized vehicle. Mae clutches her bag and heads for the change room we passed as we walked to the beach. I, on the other hand, not far off buck naked, have no choice but to race to the sand-smeared boxers and gracelessly dance my way into them. Just in time.

Uncomfortably gritty though they are, the form-fitting Manmade boxer briefs can pass for swim trunks, from a distance. By the time the ATV gets to me, I am fully clothed, minus footgear.

The two local laddios are smiling. Cheeky teenagers, likely still in high school.

'Hello, guys. What's up?' Straight out and energetic, my embarrassment firmly under wraps.

They don't buy it. 'Wouldn't catch me in that water,' says one.

The other fellow can't resist. 'Cold enough to freeze the balls off a brass monkey.'

They have their chuckle.

'Where you from?' one asks.

'St. John's.'

'That explains it.' Another chuckle. 'All the same, I give it to you and the missus. That took guts.'

The "missus" appears, fully dressed, hair noticeably wet.

'Well, hello, b'ys,' she says. 'Whaddya at?' Deliberately heavy on the accent.

Mae's caught them off guard. They're not sure if she's having them on.

'You lives close by,' she says, 'so now then, b'ys, what can you tell us about Lord's Cove?'

For the moment they're lost for a response. 'Nothin' much happens in Lord's Cove.'

'I'm talking a hundred years ago,' she says.

It takes a few seconds. 'You means the tsunami?'

That's exactly what she means. The chat has taken a ninety-degree turn.

'Not many places can say it took a direct hit by a tsunami,' I point out.

It was 1929 and something unprecedented in Newfoundland—a major earthquake, roughly three hundred kilometres offshore. Two and a half hours later the seawater receded, and then, within minutes, three enormous waves struck land, ripping apart homes and fishing premises, washing them out to sea, turning the southern Burin Peninsula into a scene of massive destruction. The merciless tsunami snatched away twenty-eight lives.

Including a mother and three of her children in Lord's Cove, we're now told. One of the fellows remembers hearing the story firsthand as a boy, from his great-grandmother.

'They all drowned when the house was smacked off its foundation and into the harbour by one wave, then smacked back to shore with another. Ended up in a pond, half underwater. When they got to the house the four of them on the ground floor was dead. But when they had a look upstairs, there was another one of the youngsters, still alive in her crib.'

The lads know the story well. Sharing it changes the mood of our encounter, which, as an ex-history teacher, I'm thrilled to see. It refutes the vision we have of teenagers not thinking beyond themselves and their peers, and hardly beyond the past twenty-four hours.

'You've seen the pictures?' he adds. 'Unbelievable, eh?'

It comes with a sense of pride that the community recovered in the way that it did. Rebuilt and forged ahead. Yes, we've seen those pictures, too.

'B'ys, thanks for filling us in,' Mae says.

'No sweat.'

The two of them look at each other, pleased with themselves. Then, grinning, they turn to me. 'We didn't really think you was an exhibitionist.'

Of the three, Mae laughs the loudest.

They're back on their ATV. They tear off to a clear stretch of sand, cut a pair of donuts, then boot it back up the road, having added more circles to the dozens of others scattered across the beach.

It's late in the day by the time we arrive in Grand Bank. It's here we'll spend the night, and tomorrow afternoon we'll drive to nearby Fortune and catch the ferry to Saint-Pierre.

It's Mae's first time in Grand Bank. I have a ready recipient for my enthusiasm. We head to Abbie's Garden B & B, check in with the delightful owner, Donna, and her dog, then grab a supper of fish and chips at the Copper Kettle Café, before setting out to explore the centre of town.

Our walk takes us to the Mariners' Memorial Garden and the life-size bronze statue standing on the other side of a circular pool of water in front of us. She is the woman, the mother, the widow, gripping a handrail, strained by the agonizing memory of the countless seafarers who ventured out from their communities, never to return. The engraved names of some of them lie submerged in the water below. The memorial is the work of sculptor Luben Boykov.

Today has been a succession of rather bleak but inspiring encounters with Newfoundland history. That's me, that's what I'm about. I go to a place on holiday, I want to experience the stories behind it. As I have been known to say, R and R only takes me so far.

Not to say I can't chill on the deck off our room this evening, especially with a glass of wine and the homemade chocolate cheesecake (topped with chocolate sauce, whipped cream, and blueberries) that Donna personally delivered as a surprise treat for her guests.

Winding down, revisiting the day, anticipating tomorrow's storyline.

Mae has yet to complain about my compulsion for the past. She seems willing to embrace it, in fact. Well . . . maybe "embrace" is too strong a word. But there it is. We both know what we signed up for when our relationship ventured into the long term.

'I'm really looking forward to Saint-Pierre,' she notes. 'I'm excited.'

She's been there once before. On a school trip in junior high. My ex and I also ventured to the island. Not long after we were married, before Nick came along.

In both our cases, now pretty much a blur. Except, for some reason, we have definite memories of the *pâtisseries*. Thirty years ago, coming from Newfoundland, we thought croissants and eclairs were exotic.

So, other than the pastries, a fresh experience. *Une nouvelle aventure* in France. What new and exotic treats await? I, too, am excited.

My phone dispenses a cost-free ring. A WhatsApp call from Nick. He's figured right, the B & B has good Wi-Fi.

'Just to let you know—I've made a reservation at Le Feu de Braise. For seven o'clock, in your name. All good.'

Notably, the last phrase is not a question. Nonetheless, I demonstrate eagerness. 'Sounds great, Nick. Sounds very French.'

He chuckles. I think he's been missing my sense of humour.

'I've invited a friend to come along. I hope you don't mind.'

A second adolescent appetite. That's stretching it. But am I about to say no? Of course not.

'His name is Zach. You'll like him.'

I'm sure I will. It would appear he's become a good friend in a short space of time.

'You guys should skip lunch,' I tell him. 'Really ramp up your hunger.' Perhaps he's been missing the sarcasm as well.

'And skip breakfast while we're at it,' he says. 'Just to make it interesting.' He chuckles again.

I didn't raise the kid to outsmart his father. 'Can't wait until you graduate and start earning the big bucks. What wildly extravagant meals are in my future!'

'Dream on, *Papa*.'

'See you tomorrow.'

'*Salut*. Cheers.'

(Which reminds me—that upsurge in his taste in wine? Another boost to the restaurant tab.)

DEUX

AT THE DINING room table in the morning my self-restraint is under siege. Fortunately, before listing the array of breakfast choices, Donna places a glistening dish of fresh fruit and berries in front of each of us. I savour every nutritious piece. It offsets the guilt, leaving me to partake wholeheartedly in the bacon, eggs, and maple syrup-soaked pancakes, all the way to the scone slathered in homemade blackberry jelly.

A breakfast to power us through the former Yugoslav Pavilion from Expo 67.

I love this underappreciated fact.

'Remember all those wonderful pavilions that filled the site of the Montreal world's fair in 1967?' I say cheerily as we're driving toward the heart of Grand Bank.

'A bit before my time.'

'Mine, too.' Which, however, was no hindrance to discovering yet another fascinating sidenote to our history.

'After the fair ended, the vast majority of the pavilions were demolished and carted off to landfills. Not so the pavilion from Yugoslavia. A deal was cut with the Government of Newfoundland, the structure dismantled, shipped to the port of Botwood, and trucked to Grand Bank, where it was reassembled, retro-fitted, and winterized into—ta-dah—the Provincial Seamen's Museum.'

We've just pulled into its parking lot. Impeccable timing.

'Wow,' she says. 'Surreal.'

'Don't you love how the huge triangular components just sailed in and transplanted themselves onto the landscape.'

They look like schooner sails, just as the politicians eager to finalize the deal pointed out. Absolutely. My imagination has no trouble making the leap, despite it being a windless day as we exit the car and stroll toward the museum.

'Not like you to be stuck in the doldrums,' Mae says, as she leads the way inside. She's not done with me yet. She chuckles and holds the door open.

'An underinflated wit,' I say as I step past her.

It's shortly after ten. The museum has only just opened. The young woman behind the admissions desk is pleased to see such a buoyant couple as the first visitors for the day.

As I swipe my credit card, she inquires, 'Would you mind if I ask where you folks are from? The museum keeps a record.'

'Not far, I'm afraid. St. John's.'

'No problem. They all count.'

I'm sure she didn't mean to sound quite so underwhelmed. 'Not so long ago I spent a few days in Mexico,' I tell her, 'if that's of any help.'

My deadpan expression puts her off. 'I'm afraid not.'

Mae catches her eye, relieving the young woman of the suspicion she might have a nutjob on her hands.

'*No hay problema*,' I add, surprised I even remember the phrase.

Mae digs me in the ribs. 'The next time I'll leave him at home.'

I look across the desk, my hands raised in mock surprise. I'm tempted to wink at the young woman, but these days I know better. I walk away expressionless, chuckling only when we're out of her sight.

'Sebastian . . . the poor girl . . .'

'It relieves her boredom. Keeps her on her toes. I was doing her employer a service.'

Mae knows there's no point. She turns her attention to the museum's artifacts. Many of them date from a time that saw dozens of schooners go out from the harbours of the Burin Peninsula to fish the Grand Banks, men sent over the sides to handline for cod in dories, two-man open boats tossed about in fog and unpredictable seas.

The hour-long tour is starkly uplifting, reinforcing the pride I feel in our centuries-old seafaring past.

The young woman at the admissions desk sets aside her cellphone as we approach her at the end of our visit. 'We're so pleased we came. *Muchas gracias.*'

'Would you like to sign the visitor's book?' she inquires, somewhat tentatively.

For certain. I'm fully aware that a well-used visitor's book in a local museum helps keep the government dollars flowing.

"*¡Fantástico!*" I write with a flourish, then sign my name. That inverted exclamation mark is sure to grab her attention, offset her bias against my hometown, the name of which I add with an equal flourish.

I scan the page and the one before it to see what exotic places other visitors happen to call home. How about Bangor, Maine? Sigh. Or Dundas, Ontario? Yawn. How about Mount Pearl . . .

I'm just about to roll my eyes when "Les Trois-Îlets, Martinique" springs from the page.

Preceded by the name of its resident—Philippe Jean. And his comment—"*Merci pour cette belle visite. Super! Merveilleux!*"

I point it out to Mae as I move aside to give her space to sign the book. The fashion designer managed to squeeze in a visit to the Seamen's Museum in Grand Bank before boarding the ferry to Saint-Pierre. 'Well now, isn't that a coincidence.'

'The man gets around,' says Mae.

Our exchange has aroused the curiosity of the young woman behind the admissions desk.

'We're thinking the museum doesn't get many visitors from Martinique.'

'You must mean Philippe. He's the first, as far as I know. I had to ask him where Martinique is, exactly.'

I'm curious. The Newfoundland museum attendant and the Caribbean visitor—chatty to the point they were quickly on a first-name basis.

The young woman turns her head to one side, drawing a hand to the fabric that ties together her shoulder-length hair.

'Philippe gave me this. It's a summer neck gaiter really, but it doubles as a headband or a scrunchie.'

Well, you live and learn. A neck gaiter reborn as a scrunchie. Bright, multicoloured, in a pattern that I'm guessing is tropical plants. It would seem Philippe had a stockpile of gifts he handed out to new acquaintances. The Burin Peninsula may well be dotted with Caribbean fashion accessories.

'Very nice,' says Mae. 'It suits your hair colour.'

'Philippe chose it carefully. He had several in his backpack.'

I was wondering where the stockpile was housed. And what other curiosities might have been contained therein. Scarves, wristbands, tote bags—no end to the possibilities.

Our conversation with the young woman (still nameless to us) has reached its logical endpoint. Nothing more to add, except a rather colourless, 'Thanks again. We hope you enjoy the rest of your day.'

'*Bon voyage*,' she says, suddenly chirpy as we're going out the door.

Fortune, our gateway to Saint-Pierre, awaits.

Fortunately I've purchased the ferry tickets online, so by the time I've parked the car in the storage lot and the attendant drives us and our luggage back to the ferry terminal, we have a solid five minutes to sit and gather our thoughts before hearing the announcement to board the *Nordet.*

'Cutting it a bit close,' Mae remarks.

'I'd call it perfect timing.' Perspective is everything.

All good. We're aboard and settled into one of the lounges, with an agreeable view through the window as the mooring lines are released and the ship manoeuvres out the harbour.

I text Nick to let him know we're on our way, a final message before Mae and I double-check that the international roaming plans we bought for our phones are activated, for when we can't use WhatsApp. In just over an hour we'll be setting foot in *la France.*

Vive la France! It has a historic resonance, an allure, an intrigue. In my mind a *mélange* of baguettes, camembert, Pinot Noir, and Marion Cotillard. Mae agrees she was brilliant in *La Vie en Rose*, and that no one has ever had a voice quite like Edith Piaf.

In other words, we're flying high and in perfect sync as we head for the deck to take in the craggy outer islands of Saint-Pierre, and the iconic *pointe aux Canons* lighthouse that marks the entrance to the harbour. And, inland, the maze of narrow streets with their restaurants and bars, their *pâtisseries*, *épiceries*, and *boulangeries*, and heaven only knows what else eager to invigorate the anglophone palate.

As we reach the pier, a dockhand secures the vessel's mooring lines. In the distance, beyond the security fence, Nick is waving a hand above his head. We wave back before quickly heading to the stairs that take us down to the disembarkation level. We collect our luggage and slip into the lineup for the customs kiosks.

The agent is pleased that ours is more than a quick weekend visit. He hands us back our passports. '*Bienvenue à SPM, les îles de Saint-Pierre-et-Miquelon.*'

'*Merci, monsieur.*'

'*Bonne journée,*' adds Mae.

Yes, my friend, we're here to immerse ourselves, not whip in and out and check it off some superficial bucket list.

Nick greets us excitedly. He hugs me, all vim and vigour.

'*Il est tout excité,*' as we say in France or, more precisely, as Mae whispers to me, with Nick just ahead, wheeling our luggage to the van that's waiting for us.

'*Bienvenue*, I'm Pascal.'

I've corresponded with Pascal, the owner of Auberge Daguerre. It's a great service, so much better than having to round up a taxi. Pascal is good-humoured and engaging, speaking to both of us in English and Nick in French once he realizes he's a student at the Francoforum.

We all board the van for the five-minute drive to the inn, Nick in the front passenger seat, chatting up a French storm, proud dad behind catching the odd phrase. *C'est la vie.* Besides, my high school French and the university course I did thirty years ago are bound to kick in sooner rather than later.

Nick waits in the sitting room of the inn, adjacent to the registration desk. Mae and I head up the stairs to drop our luggage and check out the room. All's looking very good, including a welcoming bottle of wine and an assortment of chocolates, and the king-size bed with its cluster of decorative pillows. (Useless as pillows, of course, but a seductive touch.) We are soon downstairs again, ready to head off with Nick for a walk about town prior to dinner at seven at Le Feu de Braise.

Saint-Pierre has noticeably changed since I was last here. Its infrastructure has been upgraded, its recreation and cultural facilities expanded. The Old World charm is still there, but the town's more polished.

That's what money from the mother country can do for an outpost floating alone on the other side of the Atlantic Ocean. France provides a strong financial foundation to Saint-Pierre and Miquelon. It likes making a showcase, small though it is, of its North American territory.

'*Collectivité d'outre-mer,*' Nick informs us.

I make a valid attempt to get my tongue round it.

'Good try,' he says, almost under his breath.

Apparently he feels condescension comes off better in his native language. On the positive side, I see a willingness to accommodate his father's unilingual tendencies.

'Only when there's no *Saint-Pierrais* close by,' he points out, only marginally louder.

By which he means the local residents, who by now have figured out he must be in the fall term at the Francoforum, one of the new batch of students boning up on their French, who are expected to speak it everywhere they go, without exception.

'I don't want to get caught out. It doesn't look good. On us or the program.'

From what I've heard of his French so far, there's little chance of that happening. He's arrived well prepared with a solid background in the language, having done advanced courses in high school and university. Plus, the dude is not lacking in confidence.

We seat ourselves on a park bench in the *place du Général de Gaulle*. It's near the harbour, a central plaza, with no local residents within yelling distance. In other words, my English tongue has carte blanche.

'You know of course that the man himself stood in this very plaza in 1967.'

Of course he didn't.

'The general had a soft spot for your *Saint-Pierrais*. During World War II they declared themselves in support of de Gaulle's Free French Forces. Canada and the States, on the other hand, were sticking by the Vichy government in France, which had signed an armistice with the invading Germans, but was really collaborating with them.'

If I'm sounding orally unleashed it's because I am. Single track, no double talk—a history addict with a story that begs no translation.

'De Gaulle wanted his Free France Navy to take control of the islands. Canada and the United States argued vehemently against it. The irrepressible general ignored them and plunged ahead.

'On the night of December 23, 1941, three Free France corvettes and a submarine slipped into the harbour. An armed landing party stormed ashore. Right where we are now. The administrator was captured, the upstarts seized control of the islands. Citizens poured onto the streets and delivered them a hero's welcome. Not a shot was fired. A plebiscite on Christmas Day declared victory—over ninety per cent of the population voting in favour of de Gaulle and his Free France Forces. A small but very symbolic victory. A tour de force!'

'*Vive le Saint-Pierre libre!*'

Brilliant. No flies on Mae.

The lad is too young to get her riff on de Gaulle's infamous declaration when he visited Quebec four days later.

'*Vive le Québec libre!*' Nick declares.

Right. I forgot. He did get an A in Canadian History in high school.

I can do him one better. 'It was de Gaulle who also said, "The better I get to know men, the more I find myself loving dogs."'

'Sweet,' says Nick. He smiles broadly. Not without a touch of melancholy. Suddenly we're both thinking about Gaffer.

Mae looks as if she's about to roll her eyes. As much as she loves Gaffer, she doesn't truly appreciate our sudden yearning for the mutt's tongue in our faces, a warp speed wag of his tail. She injects, 'It was de Gaulle who also said, "How can you govern a country that has 246 varieties of cheese?"'

As a tactic to get us back on track, it fails. 'Gaffer loves brie.'

'Remember when he stole that wedge of comté and ate it all?' says Nick.

A favourite flashback for us both. 'Even though he threw up most of it.'

'Okay, you guys. Enough with the dog craving. Time to move on.'

Reluctantly. Nick suggests we transition to Le CIA, a gourmet food and wine shop on *rue Albert Briand*, the same street as Le Feu de Braise. 'The perfect place to kill time before the restaurant opens for dinner.'

He's right. The shop's specialty is French wine. No surprise there. A selection that far outshines anything we can get back home, and at a much better bang for the euro. Wicked. Plus, there's the stellar range of *rhum agricole* from the French Caribbean. Unfortunately (or fortunately, considering my cash flow) I'm not much of a rum drinker.

And then there's the Scotch. Not a bad selection, although not such a great deal as the wine, the whisky being born and bred in Scotland, not *la France.* There's a Highland Park that I haven't seen before. I take out my phone and do a quick background check. Reviews leave it dead in the glass. And something called Smokehead, with in-your-face packaging and a price that deactivates any interest I might have. I grab a couple of pictures, on the off chance I have second thoughts.

Nick gestures for me to join him. He points to a naked bottle called Henri's Legacy.

'You're kidding.'

A whisky "originally handcrafted" in Saint-Pierre and Miquelon, verified by the map on the label. A label in English, presumably to appeal to an international market. Which would be me.

I'm not so sure. To begin with, it doesn't come in a box or tube. (The whisky snob in me is surfacing.) Secondly, the label also says "new make." Not something to get me excited.

There's whisky and then there's exceptional whisky. I'm never quick to fork over the cash if it's for something I know nothing about.

'I'll need to taste it first,' I tell Nick.

'It's not bad,' he whispers.

I curb my surprise. I gather that in addition to wine, and to beer and shooters, the young man is spending his limited pocket money on whisky. That says something. Something about being tarred with the same brush.

In the meantime, Mae is checking out the food. We divert our collective attention to what she might have discovered. It appears the shop is particularly well stocked with canned products from the Basque country. Not surprising, given the historical connection between it and Saint-Pierre and Miquelon.

Such things as cans of green olives stuffed with *saumon, citron et aneth*. I'll love any stuffed olive, even if it is with *aneth*.

And cans of *chipirons*. What I first bet were sardines are actually small squid. Stuffed in a sardine-sized can. 'Whole and packed in Basquaise sauce,' Mae points out, having taken a closer look at the label. (The Basque are very big on sauces, it seems.)

I'm sure I'll love a good saucy miniature squid. Especially since Mae has placed four cans of them on the counter next to the cash register. They are in short supply and she doesn't want to risk the little devils not being there when she returns to the shop later in the week for the wine she'll also be bringing back home.

With the stockpile paid for and slipped into her tote, we're out the door and back to *rue Albert Briand*. The restaurant is just opening up for the evening.

'Zach,' calls Nick, whom he's spotted waiting to one side of the entrance. Nick makes a quick check for *Saint-Pierrais*.

'Come meet my dad. And my dad's friend.' Nick's never been sure how to refer to Mae.

Zach is slightly shorter than Nick, but otherwise they're much alike. Similar builds, on the lean side. Hair longish on top and close cropped on the sides. Dressed not quite warmly enough for fall. Unlike Nick, Zach wears glasses—round with tortoise shell frames. Retro I would say, and trendy.

I hold out my hand. 'Sebastian.' He shakes it firmly.

He's enthusiastic, if self-conscious. 'Nick has told me a lot about you.'

I assume it's positive, as confirmed by Nick, though his smile has a taunting edge to it. I would say any comments Nick might have made to his friend were coloured with stories of our head-butting once adolescence took hold. Par for the course. And well behind us now.

Nick introduces Mae. '*Salut, ça va?*' she says. Naturally charming without any effort.

'*Ça va bien, merci.*'

Fortunately, once we're inside we're directed to a table at enough distance from the other patrons that my own *je ne sais quoi* can take hold.

'So, Zach, where were you cooked up, as Nick once said to me, jokingly of course.'

Nick looks at Zach. 'I told you.'

'Sebastian,' cautions Mae.

Zach is amused, not the least bit fazed. Give the guy credit.

'No, really,' I say, 'where did you grow up?' To appease the others.

'Baytona.'

I'm tempted to smile, even laugh. I glance at Nick. He's deadpan. He knows Baytona makes me cringe every time I hear it. Daytona with a B. So not-Newfoundland it's embarrassing.

I'm guessing Zach is having me on. I'm guessing Nick put him up to it. But I'm not sure I want to take that chance.

'Really?'

'It used to be called Gayside,' says Zach.

Exactly. 'It was changed sometime in the 1980s, as I recall. Before you were born.'

'Oddly enough, yes.' Pause. He breaks out laughing. Another pause, long enough to add, 'Actually, I grew up in Lamaline.'

Nick roars. The buggers.

'That deserves a drink,' says Mae, as openly amused as the other two. She scans the bar list before passing it on. 'I'm going to have a Cosmopolitan.'

Very good. Sounds sophisticated. Makes for a welcome enrichment of the conversation.

'What's on tap?' I ask, as Nick looks over the list. Guys that age all love their beer.

He takes his time. 'Actually, I'm thinking martini.'

A martini? I doubt if he's ever had a martini. But why not up his drinks game free of charge.

'I think I'll try a whisky,' says Zach.

I glance at Nick. I suspect he's put Zach up to it. Set him in sync with my passion for the dram.

'How about you both have a shot of Henri's Legacy?' says Nick. 'It's on the list. You could compare tasting notes.'

'I'm game,' says Zach.

Which means I'm also game, as orchestrated by my wily son.

In due course the drinks arrive—the Cosmopolitan, decidedly pink and frothy, and the martini, clear and bearing an olive, hopefully Basque. The whisky, iceless as requested, but not in proper whisky glasses.

That said, whisky is all about the pure, unadorned glazing of the taste buds. Zach and I clink glasses and give it a go.

As I suspected, "new make" is in need of more time in the barrel if it's going to reach the stage where I can get beyond "not bad."

Zach, who I assume has had limited exposure to whisky, or none at all, is unsure what to say. 'I think I like it. I don't have much to compare it to.'

'It takes time,' I tell him. 'This is a reasonable starting point. You work your way up from here.'

'The other day in the Super U, I came across a whisky made in France. It's called *Eddu*. Have you heard of it?'

So. His interest is for real. I shouldn't be surprised. I've noticed over the past few years at WhiskyFest there's been a slew of cool young dudes. Hardly shaving and they're lining up for a sip of Ardbeg Uigeadail. (And even knowing how to pronounce it.)

'I have heard of it. Before I came on this trip I researched French whiskies. *Eddu* is made in Brittany. The distillery was the first in the world to produce whisky from buckwheat. Rather radical, but worth a try.'

Not that I necessarily expected to find *Eddu* in Saint-Pierre. Especially not in a shop with such a banal, characterless name.

'Super U's a supermarket,' Nick informs me, before I can comment.

On the one hand it's refreshing that the sale of whisky is not restricted to government-run outlets, as it is in most of Canada. But, on the other, seeing an artfully boxed, beautifully aged whisky wedged in your grocery cart between the laundry detergent and a bag of potatoes doesn't exactly add to the thrill of acquisition.

'I'm thinking I might buy a bottle,' Zach says, 'although I really can't afford it.'

Which is also refreshing. I look over at Nick and smile. 'Budgeting is a skill not to be dismissed.' Tempted as he might be, Nick holds himself in check.

My advice to Zach is to first spend some time checking out what else is available at the various shops around town. 'Take pictures. Compare reviews online. Make a list. The anticipation of finding a good dram at a decent price is half the fun.'

'I'm working on an essay about smuggling booze from Saint-Pierre. I like the idea of chilling out with a whisky when I'm done for the night. It doesn't have to be French, because of course most of what was smuggled during Prohibition was Canadian. But you know, I can't see myself sipping on Canadian Club.'

Wise beyond his years. How about unconventional, non-conformist? I'm enjoying this fellow.

But I need more background. I thought he was here solely for the French courses. He now tells me his minor is French, that he's actually majoring in history, and while in Saint-Pierre he's also working on a research project as part of his honours history degree, one that requires writing an essay about his findings.

A history major talking to an ex-history teacher. How about that. We've struck very common ground.

'I would have thought the story of smuggling into the States from Saint-Pierre during Prohibition was already well documented.'

'I'm taking a different angle,' he tells me. 'I'm still in the process of working it out.'

Exactly what angle he doesn't say.

I understand the reluctance. For now, it's enough just to sit there and admire his ambition. Honours program—impressive. His brain is firing on all cylinders, as they say.

Nick is getting a charge out of the fact that Zach and I have hit it off. The truth is I'd have to go back a few years to find friends of Nick's I haven't liked. Which, if I'm reading that right, tells me father and son are on much the same wavelength, that we get along for good reasons.

All this is going through my head as we share an entrée of Miquelon-produced *foie gras de canard*, with rhubarb chutney. And then again when Nick and I are both tucking into *magret de canard, sauce miel et gingembre*. We had scoured the menu with its array of *les plats*, all tempting, but, without any discussion between us, had both settled on the duck.

Nick looks at me and grins. It's triggered a memory. For years not an especially good one, although we laugh about it now. It takes us back to our first Christmas after his mother and I separated.

It was a bit of a rough time for us both, given he spent the whole of Christmas Day at his mother's. I decided to go all out, making his Boxing Day meal at my place one he wouldn't soon forget.

Which turned out to be the case. The duck came out of the oven overcooked, charred in fact. Since he was studying French in school, I thought carrots and parsnip *à la Vichy* would be a winner. (He took his time picking past the parsnip to get to the carrots.) The *freekeh* pistachio salad proved to be a bit freakish for a twelve-year old. And as for dessert—it was ambitious on my part, but I knew he loved tiramisu. He quietly noted he preferred the Costco version.

At the time the meal wasn't much of a cause for celebration. Nonetheless, there was nowhere to go but up, and in the years following we've bonded over dozens of meals we've cooked together, and which, I will add, were generally memorable for the right reasons.

The French have a way with duck, as they do with Mae's choice of shrimp (*flambées au Ricard*) and Zach's veal (*flambée au Calvados*).

And, needless to say, as they do with the glasses of white and red that flow freely. We're glowing.

I save my *flambée* for dessert—*mirabelles de Lorraine* afire over *crêpes Mylene*. A mouthful in more ways than one. Delicious. In the meantime, the lads effortlessly take to crème brûlée, while Mae takes a pass.

Nick is already looking past dessert to see if there is any section of the menu we haven't hit. 'How about *les digestifs*?'

Why not? My credit card long ago surrendered to this wide-scale attack.

Mae prefers a simple ginger tea, while the lads are liking the sound of Armagnac. The way it rolls off the tongue promises a priceless encounter with the unknown.

I smile inwardly. Young and fervent and thriving on fresh experience. I nod to the waiter for a third pour of Armagnac and raise my glass in a toast to a flamingly successful meal.

'Cheers to us all. May we prosper in body and mind. Never forgetting how fortunate we are to live in peace with good-hearted family and friends.'

I don't usually unload such sentiment, but the evening has prompted it. I look at Nick and Zach, on their own and revelling in the wider world. How good is that. What unfaltering comfort is found in having a son who has that privilege and opportunity.

Who is not expected to take up arms and go off to fight. Seriously. When I see the footage that's been dominating the news it's the first thing that hits me—how good I have it compared to what some parents are dealing with. How fortunate is the son of mine and his friends to have grown up in this time and this place.

'Cheers,' I echo.

'Thanks, Dad.' Together with the look in his eyes, it's enough.

'Thanks, Mr. Synard. I've had a great time. Can we get a group shot?'

Of course we can. Of course we can capture the moment, in a photo I expect he'll send off to his folks to let them know he's surrounded by a decent, cheerful-looking lot who treated him to a healthy meal and enjoyed his company. As a parent I would find that reassuring.

Outside the restaurant and back on *rue Albert Briand*, it's time to say goodnight and go our separate ways. They head off in the same general direction, to lodgings a few streets apart, the homes of their respective *mères françaises*. The conscientious students still have work to do in preparation for tomorrow's classes.

An endearing term—*mère française*. The woman who feeds and cares for Nick and changes his bed sheets regularly. He speaks fondly of Emmeline. We'll get the chance to meet her. She's invited us to come by for a visit.

Mae and I stroll back in the direction of our *auberge*, taking our time, enjoying the quiet of the narrow streets, unpopulated except for the occasional cat. The warmish summer evenings are long past. The football field is empty. It's a weeknight, a work and school day tomorrow. Saint-Pierre has returned to its regular self. I like experiencing a place without the face it puts together for tourists.

All's quiet at the *auberge*. We make our way wordlessly up the stairs. We shower and wrap ourselves in the thick white terrycloth robes that came with the room. We lounge about with glasses of *vin mousseux* and morsels of *chocolat noir*. Which seems all the more decadent in French.

As tempting as it is, I resist unleashing the Patti LaBelle song lyric that lies in wait in the memory bank of most men my age—*Voulez-vous coucher avec moi ce soir?* I have been waiting practically my whole life for the opportunity to use this line, yet maybe it's best not to take the chance of sounding corny and dampen her enthusiasm.

Instead, as we discard the decorative pillows and slip between the sheets, it's Edith Piaf's "*L'hymne à l'amour*" on tinny iPhone repeat. Honestly, I don't get many of the words. But then again I'm not really listening.

TROIS

LOVE A FRENCH breakfast. Love a *petit déjeuner*. To heck with the eggs and bacon and sausages. Let's go straight for the tray of pastries and select a *pain au chocolat* and one of those apple flip-ish things with the crusted sugar on top.

'*Chausson aux pommes*,' Mae informs me.

Whatever it is, it's too good to pass up. It's flipping *délicieux*.

Mae, I notice, has opted for granola and yoghurt. Which I wouldn't think is entirely authentic. It was likely added to the buffet to cater to anglophone tourists. When in Saint-Pierre, do as the *Saint-Pierrais* do, I say.

Mae does get to a pastry eventually, albeit a modest *chouquette*. Which is kinda like an undersized cream puff, without the best part—the cream.

Her restraint is pronounced, as will be mine when I get back home. I've reached a point where I'm on what I'm calling a modified version of Intermittent Fasting, where the occasional lapse is entirely manageable. Hence, on holiday, let the meals fall where they may. Embrace the moment and manage the consequences when I return home. If there are any aberrant pounds revealed by the scales, it's back on the full-force IF, and off they drop quickly and efficiently.

As we finish off our coffees we scan a map of Saint-Pierre and make plans for our morning. Mae points to *pointe du Diamant*, at the southern tip of the island, for what promises to be a scenic, nature-driven hike. With the walk to get there, it will take up the remainder of the morning. I'm already anticipating that thrill as my app leaps past the fitness sweet spot of ten thousand steps.

'What's your weekly average?'

'I don't keep track.'

'You got a boost two days ago.'

'Absolutely.'

It seems I'm expected to come up with an actual number. I hesitate to finger the icon with that loveable heart shape, but there it is, let the boosted data reveal itself and hope for the best.

'Most recent weekly average, let's see . . .' Not quite what I was hoping for. But let's keep it positive. 'And I quote, "Your step count last week was higher on average than the week before."'

'Which was?'

'Roughly in the neighbourhood of six grand.'

Her amusement only lasts so long. 'Upping your daily count by four grand should be a cinch.'

'A piece of *gâteau*.' I'm smiling.

'In other words, a *fait accompli*.'

'*Touché*.'

I think I've reached my repartee limit. *Fini* for me. Best we make a move while the going is good.

On the way out I grab a couple of apples from the buffet and slip them into my backpack. Mae is suggesting we enrich the menu selection and stop for a gourmet picnic partway through the hike. 'A bottle of Sauvignon Blanc, a freshly baked baguette, with *pâté*, brie, and *charcuterie*. And a little *je ne sais quoi* for dessert.'

Upping the step average with *panache*. Count me in.

As I remark to Mae (once we've made the last stop for provisions and have set out on the hike), I hadn't realized just how many words have been imported from French and are now common in English. 'Use them every day and you could almost sound bilingual.'

'Not quite.'

She does, however, realize the need to keep the conversation light, given what proves to be an endless walk along the *route du Cap aux Basques* to get to the actual starting point of the hike. To her way of thinking, I suspect, a healthy miscalculation.

"*Route*" should have been my first clue. As compared to "*rue*," the word has a certain endless quality to it. In keeping with the string of large properties and their oversize houses. (The *nouveau riche* of Saint-Pierre?) Yet I'm not about to outwardly complain. In fact, as the steps burgeon along the *route du Cap aux Basques* I can only think the magic ten thousand will be signed, sealed, and delivered before we even reach the starting point. Then more than doubled, since after we do the elusive *pointe du Diamant* hike we have to make our way all the way back to town.

Ah, is that not a point of land I see in the distance, jutting into the ocean, looking so very hike-worthy? As we draw nearer, there, proudly upright, is the sign we have both been waiting for, depicting a person decked in hiking gear, walking stick in full motion. No translation needed.

And not only that, but a hike prep station. And no ordinary outhouse at that. In Newfoundland we have come to tolerate the putrid, claustrophobic shed where one is forced to do one's business. Now before me stands what amounts to a compact Quonset hut with a major league ventilation system at one end. And inside—good God, room enough to hold a dance party, which is what you want in celebration of the fact that the air is breathable. Got to hand it to the French. When nature calls, they answer with class.

And as for the hike, it is all that Mae proposed it would be—rugged oceanscape, accessible by rustic, sturdy boardwalk. Eleven thousand, one hundred and four steps to get us there. Well worth it, but it's stirred up an appetite.

We sidestep the picnic table for seats on a cluster of boulders, a more elemental, *en plein air* experience. Fine dining on the *Diamant* rocks. A one-star Michelin at least.

I'm just into my second paper cup of wine when my phone rings. It's Nick. It's 10:55. He must be between classes.

'*Bonjour, monsieur. Comment ça va?*'

'Not good,' he says abruptly.

'What's wrong?'

I detect an intake of air. 'Zach is missing.'

'What are you talking about?'

'He's disappeared.'

'What do you mean—disappeared?'

'He didn't show up for class this morning. He hasn't answered my texts. The other students where's he staying say he skipped breakfast. They figured he must have left the house early, maybe hung out in a café to work on his essay before heading to the class. I just phoned his *mère française*. She checked his room. His bed had been slept in.'

'There's got to be an explanation. He couldn't have just "disappeared."'

'It's not like Zach. He would have let someone know.'

'You're jumping to conclusions, Nick. I'll see you on your lunch break, okay. We'll come by the Francoforum. By that time you'll probably have heard from him. If not, we'll figure it out.'

'Okay,' he mutters before we disconnect.

'I don't get it,' I tell Mae. I fill in the details. 'He's overreacting.'

She holds back for a moment. 'Zach, it seems, is a very close friend.'

'They haven't known each other more than a couple of weeks.'

'Possibly more than a friend.'

It's not as if I haven't thought of that myself. 'Even so.'

I need to face that possibility. Nick, as far as I can tell, given that I'm only his father, is gay. Or possibly gay. Which, if he is, or is not, I have no problem with. That he knows, even though we've never really talked about it. What he knows is that I love him, and his sexual orientation has no bearing on that. True, I might prefer he wasn't. But that's because he might be in for a tougher time of it, since not everyone he'll meet will be open to the fact.

'You *have* talked it through?' Mae says. 'His sexuality I mean.'

'Not really talked it through, as such. But he knows how I feel.'

'You've avoided it?'

'No, I haven't avoided it. It just hasn't come up in conversation, except once when he was, like, thirteen.'

'Sebastian, Nick is nineteen, almost twenty. Believe me, Kayla and I would have had that discussion long before now.'

Kayla is her daughter who has just graduated from university. Whole different situation. 'She's a girl. Mothers and daughters are different.'

'That's crap.'

Really? That's being sensitive? I don't say anything.

'You know what I mean.'

I don't care to know, actually. I'm somewhat pissed off, and she can see that.

'I'm sorry. He's your son. You interact differently.'

I still don't say anything. Nick and I have it together. We can read each other's minds without having to put it into words. With the divorce we've been through a lot of shit. We've made it work.

'I'm sorry,' she says again. 'I shouldn't get involved.'

Which is true. 'No problem.' Which is not quite the same as accepting her apology, but it's as close as it's likely to get, at this point at least.

It puts an unavoidable drag on the remainder of the hike. I should be able to let it go, but for whatever reason it's not happening.

I do a reasonable job of faking it. We chat as we make our way back into Saint-Pierre, fortunately by a different route, with unfamiliar surroundings that bear comment. When the Francoforum finally comes into view it's a relief for us both.

'Look at that,' I say, checking the number of steps that have been piling up, regardless of my brooding stride. 'Twenty-five thousand and counting.'

'A personal best, would you say?'

I wouldn't say anything. It is what it is. I shrug. As I said before, I haven't kept track.

She's likely thinking my reaction has a ring of petulance. That's her choice.

The sight of Nick puts an end to that train of thought. He's waiting impatiently outside the front entrance.

'Zach is still not answering my texts. I figure he's on Île aux Marins. C'mon, we got to make the 1:30 ferry.'

He blurts out an explanation as we're hurrying toward the docks.

'It's an island in the harbour. People lived on it one time. It was resettled in the 1960s. Zach and I have been there before.'

Both Mae and I have read about Île aux Marins. Several of the original buildings are still there, well maintained, giving a sense of the island as it once was. It's a favourite spot for tourists, and some people from Saint-Pierre spend their summers there. We planned to visit, just not today.

'What makes you think that's where he went?' Mae asks. The point we're both wondering about.

'Research for the essay. He said he needed to go back, he just didn't say when.'

I can buy that, although it does nothing to explain why he hasn't answered Nick's texts. Maybe his phone ran out of juice.

We get to the dock with only a few minutes to spare before the ferry's departure. Following its morning runs, like most businesses in Saint-Pierre it's taken a lunch break.

Nick leads us across a short ramp to the boat. A sign next to the orange lifebuoy ring on the open deck of *Le P'tit Gravier* gives notice it can accommodate thirty-six people. The heavy summer traffic is past. I count ten of us making the crossing.

Once we're seated, the tall, dreadlocked ferry operator collects the round-trip fare, handing each of us a stub for the trip back. Nick speaks to him in French, describing Zach and, I assume, asking if he remembers him going over to the island on one of the morning crossings.

The fellow moves off to reposition the portable ramp back to the dock. He releases the mooring lines before jumping back aboard and heading to the wheelhouse.

'He thinks maybe,' Nick says. 'He can't be positive. He sees a lot of people.'

Which may have been his way of saying he was a bit hungover and doesn't remember. It seems to me we're running on speculation. There's nothing much I can do about it. I reassure Nick there's likely a simple, innocuous explanation for all this that will become apparent before long.

Mae says nothing. Her restraint says a lot. Most likely—you're the better one to deal with it, Sebastian. Anything I add will only complicate the situation.

Not entirely true, but I'm not about to go there at the moment.

The crossing takes fifteen minutes, most of it within sight of the island. I try to divert Nick's attention by pointing to various structures as they come into view. 'That must be the church. And there's the lighthouse.'

'What was your first clue?' he says, grim-faced.

I ignore it, adding, 'Deactivated, I would think.'

'Resettlement has that effect.'

I welcome the drollness, shrouded though it is. I'm inclined to put an arm around his shoulder, but think better of it.

We disembark, ready for confirmation that Zach is somewhere on the island. Our strategy for finding him rests with Nick, who seems very definite about the route he wants to take.

At first our destination appears to be the church, but we suddenly veer left and toward the northern end of the island. Through open fields, past a few rustic dwellings well off the path. We soon see the last of them. I expect that once we're up and over the incline ahead there'll be nothing but grass and rocks and shoreline.

Not so. The landscape is abruptly filled with a large, decidedly turquoise two-storey box with a parade of undersized windows. As architecture goes, flatly utilitarian and a bit bizarre.

'*Qu'est-ce que c'est?*' says Mae.

'Chez Anne-Laure,' Nick tells us. 'Zach was fascinated with this place. Not what it is now, what it once was.'

According to Nick what it is now is a guesthouse, a hostel of sorts, often catering to young travellers.

'Zach came to Saint-Pierre a couple of days before the start of the semester to do research for his essay. He stayed here. Maybe he came back.'

Which makes absolutely no sense. It was close to nine o'clock last night when Zach was last seen in Saint-Pierre. It was dark, the ferry had long stopped. No way was he going to turn up at Chez Anne-Laure. Even if for some unknown reason he made it look like the bed in his boarding house had been slept in.

Yet Nick is determined to find out for sure. Stairs lead to a veranda and a front entrance, but there's also a back deck at ground level with a door that seems the one in common use. Mae and I stay on the path while Nick heads toward it.

He returns despondent. 'The supervisor remembered Zach. She hasn't seen him since.'

We walk on. The landform changes suddenly, narrowing to an isthmus that separates a broad cove and beach on one side, a straighter rocky shoreline on the other. At its end the isthmus widens into green, craggy terrain, an uphill expanse capped by a huge bald rock.

'The highest point of land on the island,' Nick says, without any enthusiasm.

There's more to capture attention. Most prominently a rusted bow of a ship sunk into the shoreline rocks, all that's left, Nick says, of the *Transpacific*, a cargo ship that ran aground on a nearby reef fifty years ago. The ship was abandoned. The local fishermen helped themselves to anything they could lay their hands on—food, engines, lawn mowers, juke boxes . . .

'Zach loved that story. Especially the bit about the juke boxes.'

Nick is lost in thought, as if remembering something. He walks on by himself, in the other direction.

'You're right. Zach was more than a friend.'

Mae doesn't say anything for a moment. She holds my hand between both of hers.

We approach Nick on the beach, arms folded, staring out at the water. The sun is shining, but still, it's September. He's taken off his hoodie and his Blundstones and set them aside on the sand. In a T-shirt and rolled-up jeans he looks as if he's about to walk into the saltwater.

'Believe me, it's a lot colder than it looks.'

'We're into cold-water swimming. Zach calls it being in his blue space.'

Seriously? Blue space?

'You mean you two have been here before? Swimming?'

'We really got off on this beach.'

Mae doesn't think it's so strange. Which, of course, doesn't surprise me, given our beach experience a couple of days ago. 'It's been proven to be very good for your spiritual and mental health.'

But not so good for your physical health. Especially if you hang in there for long. 'I hope you're being careful.' Which is the most I can say since I'm no longer sanctioned to stand guard over my son. They go off into the world and you hope the hell they have sense enough to stay safe.

'No chance of broken bones,' he says. A not-so-subtle reference to a fall of several metres and the now infamous steel pin in my femur.

'Just saying,' I counter.

'We know our boundaries.'

I appreciate the sound of that. Self-imposed boundaries have a mature ring to them.

Nick walks into the cold water, without flinching. Not far, just up to the edge of his jeans. And stands there, looking out. There's nothing much to see except for the rocky, uninhabited fringes of Saint-Pierre in the distance, barren hillsides holding a single communications tower.

Nick is obviously trying to process what he should do next. Frankly I see no point in sticking around Île aux Marins. It's obvious that Zach didn't show up here. Let Nick have his moment. When he's ready we'll head back and catch the return ferry.

The best thing Mae and I can do for the moment is give him some space. We look at each other and nod, then turn and begin a slow walk farther along the beach.

The beach is made up of coarse sand, with small rocks, rounded over time, scattered through it. The rocks gradually increase in size and number until they cover the sand completely.

Seawater has lapped over some of them, brightening their reddish orange tint.

At the end of the beach, before it gives way to the grassy slope and its prodigious rock, the foreshore is abruptly coated with a wide expanse of seaweed—thick clumps of kelp, mounded over what I assume are boulders. The glistening green and yellow fronds undulate with the seawater making its way to shore. Rather surreal, like thick flowing strands of hair.

'Oh, Jesus!'

Mae grabs my arm and holds it fiercely tight.

'Do you see it!'

'See what?'

Only now coming into my sightline, is—oh, Jesus!—someone's head and shoulders! Face down between two large clumps of kelp. The rest of the body appearing to be sunk into a shallow pool between the boulders and covered by the seaweed.

Nick comes running. I blunt his stride. He doesn't need this.

He pushes past me. 'What's going on!?' He sees what we've seen and halts abruptly. 'No!'

We dread the worst. And are now driven to prove it wrong. I get rid of my hiking shoes and socks and stupidly roll up my pants.

The kelp is slippery as hell. Nick and I walk tentatively between the boulders, pressing the seaweed into the sand beneath it, holding each other upright until we reach the body. Bending down, we sweep aside the fronds, revealing the feet and legs.

And then his swim trunks. 'It can't be him,' says Nick. 'Those are not his.'

The trunks are brightly coloured, patterned with an intertwined assortment of sea creatures, in morbid contrast to the bare, ashen flesh. Whoever it is, he's undoubtedly dead.

I push aside what seaweed remains on the back. Then lift the head enough to turn it aside.

'Oh, Jesus.'

Nick falls apart.

I abandon the body, grab Nick and hold him upright.

With time we stagger back to shore. Mae wraps her arms around us both.

'I'll call 911.' I haul out my phone.

'1-1-2,' Mae mutters.

I don't understand.

'France. A different emergency number.'

Nick retrieves his phone, ignoring me. He punches in the number. He reaches *la gendarmerie*. His French is halting but he's understood.

It sounds as if the police want more detail. Nick struggles, but when the call is over he appears to have answered their questions. 'They're on their way.'

It takes time. The wait is framed by indecision. Nick is prepared for the two of us to drag the body of his friend ashore. I know it is not what the police would want, that in fact they've likely told Nick exactly that. The officer's French might have been beyond Nick's grasp. Or in his eyes it is more humane to have the body on dry land. Nevertheless, the integrity of the scene should not be compromised.

In the meantime, our activity has aroused the interest of Chez Anne-Laure. A woman is making her way briskly toward us.

She's wearing hiking boots, hiking shorts with multiple pockets, and a mustard yellow fleece. She's short, trim and fit, and to judge by her leathery tan, has lived much of her life outdoors. Attached by a lanyard around her neck is a camera. A GoPro, no less.

'Amélie Dubois,' she informs everyone before turning directly to Nick, leading me to think she's the person he talked to when he went knocking at the door of the hostel. She has yet to turn her attention to the body in the midst of the seaweed, leading me to think that even if she had binoculars, she hasn't figured out what all the commotion is about.

Nick has said little in response. He looks at me.

There's no need to tell her. She's gotten close enough to catch a glimpse of the portion of the swim trunks that failed to be covered again by seaweed once Nick and I came ashore.

'*Putain!*' she exclaims.

'The police are on their way,' I tell her. 'The *gendarmes*.'

'Dead?'

It's obvious. I say nothing.

'Are you sure?'

Amélie removes a lighter and a pack of cigarettes from a pocket of her hiking shorts and, quickly withdrawing one, lights up.

'*Qui est-ce?*' she says to no one in particular, her words trailing smoke.

Nick's halting few words are all she will get.

'*Bon Dieu de merde*,' she says.

The wait for the police is agonizing, especially for Nick. He has no wish to talk to any of us. He wanders away, retrieving his boots and hoodie. He walks to the end of the beach and begins a leaden ascent up the grassy slope toward the bald rock that defines the hillside.

I put on my socks and hiking shoes and follow behind. I stride to catch up, leaving the two women, one of whom appears ready to put her GoPro to use.

Nick has walked around to the back of the boulder and found a place to sit, looking out to sea. There is a small, uninhabited island in the distance.

I find a spot near him. He's not surprised, though he makes little effort to acknowledge me.

'He was a great guy.'

He doesn't react.

'I lost a friend years ago,' I tell him. 'His name was David. He had just graduated from university. He was killed in a motorcycle accident.'

Only now does he look at me. 'You never mentioned that before.'

'I haven't thought about it for quite a while.'

He turns away again. 'Zach and I hadn't known each other long, but we really hit it off.'

Beyond us, off from the shore, is a small island. We need the diversion.

'You came here with Zach? He was interested in that island?'

He eventually answers. 'Île aux Vainqueurs.' And eventually adds, 'A century ago it was a *lazaret*.'

"*Lazaret*" is a new one on me. I assume Nick picked it up from Zach.

'A quarantine for sailors. Yellow fever, smallpox, beriberi.'

'And Zach was particularly interested in this *lazaret?*'

'He was determined to get there. He wanted to see it for himself.'

Groundwork for his essay? Although I can't see how the island had much to do with smuggling liquor. Then again, who knows what was in Zach's mind, where his research was leading him.

It's likely we'll never know. In any case, it has faded in importance to the fact that a young man, seemingly with so much promise, has died.

'Perhaps he had a heart condition he didn't know about. Perhaps the shock of the cold water caught him unawares.'

Nick is not buying it. But we're both looking for answers. 'He'd swum in colder water. Why this time? Why now?'

'There'll be an autopsy most likely. A forensic pathologist will have some answers.'

The dispassionate terminology hits him hard.

'I'm sorry.' I move closer to him. I put an arm around his shoulder and draw us together. 'You'll get through this, pal. It'll take time, but you'll get through it.'

'Why the fuck did this happen?'

There's no answer. 'We'll find out.' I draw him tighter.

And now, in the silence surrounding us, there is distant disquiet. We emerge from behind the rock to see a boat approaching the beach. As we descend the incline the identification mark on its bow becomes clear.

SNS 160. It means nothing to me. I assume it's a boat belonging to *la gendarmerie.*

I'm wrong. '*Les Sauveteurs en Mer*,' says Amélie, with incongruous enthusiasm. I now see the words inscribed on the side of the boat's deckhouse. Amélie is waving to those on board. 'Théo! Théo!' And gesturing to the spot where the body still floats amid the seaweed.

Mae has apparently focused on the inscription since the boat first came into view, which has been long enough to input *les Sauveteurs en Mer* into Google. 'Volunteers,' she says. 'Unique to France. Tasked to save lives at sea around the French coast.'

Including the coast of Saint-Pierre and Miquelon.

'How did they know about it?' I whisper to her. 'And what the heck are they doing here before the police?'

Mae nods toward Amélie. 'From what I gather they were out on a training exercise not far from here. Her boyfriend is aboard.'

The afore-shouted Théo, I can only assume. 'But there's no life to be saved.'

'They live in hope, apparently.'

The boat releases its anchor, and only now do I notice a Zodiac trailing behind. Into it drop two crewmen in black and bright orange-red wetsuits. They are soon free of the vessel and heading to the spot Amélie is pointing to.

With her other hand she pulls an extension pole from a pocket of her shorts. Once she's sure the crewmen have sighted the body, she attaches the pole to the GoPro and raises it overhead.

The *sauveteurs* are well trained. As the Zodiac nears the broad bed of seaweed, one of the pair cuts the outboard and tilts it forward to prevent its propeller striking the rocks. Both men slip over the side and into the water, which barely reaches their knees. They pull the Zodiac atop the seaweed-covered rocks, then work their way toward the body.

They slip through the seaweed, deftly remaining upright until they reach it and stand one to each side. They are less than ten metres from the intent audience onshore that includes methodical voyeur Amélie, recording their every move.

I wonder what *la gendarmerie* would make of her efforts, given how the camera pans the whole scene, before focusing squarely on the lifesavers gripping the upper body and lifting it out of the water.

Even at eye level it's a godawful sight—the head and shoulders of a lifeless human lifted from a bed of sodden kelp.

A reveal of the brightly coloured trunks makes the view all the more freakishly aberrant. The lifesavers lower the corpse back into the water. It sinks enough that the kelp partially covers it again.

What I just witnessed, bound with good intentions though it might be, does not sit well with me. I suspect it will sit even less well with the police. A dead body has been disturbed; the scene, criminal or not, has been compromised.

Amélie, it seems, does not share my perspective.

'Théo!' she calls, having lowered her camera. 'Gabriel! *Ramenez le corps à terre.*' She is gesturing to demonstrate what route they should take, firmly pointing to the beach where we're standing. Her camera is on standby.

Boyfriend Théo and his partner Gabriel know better. Thankfully. They slowly separate themselves from the corpse and backtrack to the Zodiac. Damage done, but at least a light went on in their brains, and they retreat.

Not only retreat, but board their boat and take off out the bay, Zodiac in tow.

'Ah!' pronounces Amélie. Deflated, she uncouples the extension pole and reattaches the camera to its lanyard. It hangs listlessly at her chest.

The body has settled atop the kelp, the cloud-covered sky its only shroud.

A fragment of swimwear glares at me, shamelessly bright, near flamboyant. So much out of sorts with this place and the time of the year. It unnerves me.

It shouldn't, perhaps. Merely a carry-over from the young man's summer? A summer Nick perhaps knew little about. The brio of youth? I think long and hard . . . me, the fellow who at that age was known to parade beaches in electric blue Speedos.

Amélie is reviewing her footage. She steps closer and turns the screen to share the images, thrilled at what she has captured.

I'm even more unnerved.

The overhead angle is horridly dramatic, appearing to be footage she took after I had followed Nick up the hill. A fragment of swim trunks broadens glaringly into view.

'Stop there,' I tell Amélie. '*S'il vous plait.*'

She pauses the video. I point to the trunks, gesturing for her to enlarge the image.

The swimwear fabric fills the small but brilliant GoPro screen.

It bears a collage of intertwining sea life—crabs, lobsters, seals, whales.

And what looks to be . . . codfish? And some things triangular?

Amélie enlarges it even more. I bend slightly closer to the screen. But I need to get even closer, without infringing on her personal space.

After a motionless moment Amélie crosses herself, then bends her head downward and closes her eyes. She doesn't move a muscle. The overall experience has moved her Catholic soul to prayer, I presume.

I'm not Catholic. But I can be for the moment it takes to bend my head downward, to the side, and into the screen.

Time enough to verify what they are . . . yes, codfish. And . . . icebergs.

Ridiculously illogical for swim trunks. Not a pattern of tropical sea creatures frolicking about in a bed of coral.

But what—a pattern created especially for ice-cold water?

Bizarre. More than bizarre if you ask me.

Mae taps me on the shoulder. I was lost in thought.

As I upright myself attention shifts away from me.

It's landed on a contingent of five police officers speedily advancing along the path past Chez Anne-Laure.

Fresh off the *gendarmerie* patrol boat, I assume. Having just crossed the channel and now tied up at the dock, likely the same dock used by the ferry. In which case, I'm surprised they made it here as quickly as they did.

Single-mindedly, they strike the beach. *La Gendarmerie nationale*, only temporarily delayed, will now take charge. Looking sharp in their sky-blue jackets with the white stripe, their navy blue all-weather pants and black combat boots, sidearms in prominent view. If I were *les Sauveteurs en Mer* I'd be very glad I just reached open waters and rounded the headland, boat and Zodiac both out of sight.

'Amélie!' calls one of the officers before he reaches us.

Another couple of them acknowledge her.

'*Que s'est-il passé?*' the lead officer declares, barely breathing hard, unlike the four behind him.

It is pretty obvious what has *passé*. The young man has drowned. Amélie points to the clump of kelp where the body lies.

She reaches one hand to lift up her GoPro, but has second thoughts.

As keen as the police would be to see the video, she's cut short the move to show it to them. It's suddenly obvious to her that there's no point in getting the boyfriend involved.

In any case the scene is now very much in the hands of the five police officers. Hip waders are retrieved from a gear bag and two of them enter the water while the other three observe from shore.

Nick turns aside. He wanders away from the beach.

Mae and I follow. We, too, need a break from the overwhelming drama of the past hour.

I quietly note, 'I find police generally have an instinctual urge for secrecy.' She's surprised by the measured tone.

Not that dead bodies have become commonplace to me, but I am feeling the years of PI experience.

A prolonged, unproductive silence. I glance back to the *gendarmes* in the water. The pair have reached the corpse.

'Colonel Guy Tremblay.'

I'm surprised by the officer's quick approach.

'Commanding Officer of the *gendarmerie* of Saint-Pierre and Miquelon.'

In accented but confident English. I'm relieved.

Not only that, his name combines two hockey legends of the Montreal Canadiens during my hockey-obsessed pre-teen years: Guy Lafleur and Mario Tremblay. The colonel's name is now implanted in my mind.

He holds out his hand. I shake it and introduce myself, then the other two.

'You will need a statement from each of us.'

'Yes, but not right away. *La priorité* . . . the priority . . . excuse me . . . we will deal with the body first. I ask that the three of you come to the police station in Saint-Pierre.'

He checks his watch. 'At four o'clock. At that time we will record your statements.'

'Of course.'

'For now, Lieutenant Charpentier of *la brigade de recherches* . . .' He takes a moment to see if we all understand. 'Lieutenant Charpentier of the Investigation Unit will take your contact information. *Merci à tous.*'

He returns to the shoreline. But his spot is quickly filled.

'*Bonjour,*' with appropriate solemnity.

We respond accordingly.

'Clément Charpentier.'

A mouthful not easily replicated. I don't try, but instead introduce the three of us.

We shake hands, and then for Mae the lieutenant adds a slight nod, '*Madame.*' He begins writing in his notebook. '*Sebastien, Nicolas, et Mae,*' he demi-replicates. '*Bon.*' He seems unwilling to attempt the surnames.

'S-y-n-a-r-d,' I point out. The lieutenant is confused.

'Ess—ee-grek—en—ah—air—day,' Nick translates.

The officer turns to Mae. '*Madame?*'

She does the phonetic exposé on her surname, adding. '*En français, Lainé.*'

Not such a good idea to my mind. Why further confuse the officer?

Mae turns momentarily to me. 'I've never told you this, but my ancestors were French, from Brittany. When they settled in Newfoundland they anglicized their surname. To fit in.'

Interesting . . . but how about we save that for later. The fellow is having enough trouble as it is.

Nick thinks otherwise. He translates what Mae has said.

'*Très intéressant, madame. Très intéressant. Mon oncle habite en Bretagne.*'

'He has an uncle who lives in Brittany,' Nick tells me.

Relevant on some level, I'm sure. So, how about we go straight into addresses and cell numbers, for the sake of time?

'Ah,' the officer says to me after he's finished writing. '*Dites bonjour de ma part à Pascal.*'

I will (thanks to another translation) say hi from him to the owner of the *auberge*.

Should I be surprised he knows Pascal? Probably not.

He closes his notebook. '*Je vous retrouve tous au poste de police à seize heures.*'

Seize heures—four o'clock. At the *poste de police*. Obviously. I wave off Nick.

'*C'est bon, monsieur. Merci, monsieur.*' Even if I'm not about to take a chance on his name. The lieutenant returns to the shoreline.

'Lieutenant Clément Charpentier. KLEM-uhnt SHAAR-PON-tee-ay.' So says Nick once the officer is out of earshot.

Such patronization leads me to respond, 'You mean like Clem Carpenter.'

I shouldn't have. Nick is in no mood.

I embrace him. I can still feel the tension, but perhaps not quite as much. He hugs me back.

There's no point in remaining on the island. I lead the way back to the path and toward Chez Anne-Laure. As we are about to round the corner past it, neither of us looks back.

Police business is best left to the police. I expect no surprises. The body of Zach Russell will eventually be brought to shore and transported to Saint-Pierre and to the hospital's morgue. The Francoforum, and subsequently his parents, will be contacted and the body taken back to Newfoundland for burial. The life of a young, promising student and dear friend has ended, sad victim of recklessness in the cold seawater off the shore of Île aux Marins.

QUATRE

SURPRISE NUMBER ONE: there is no morgue in the hospital in Saint-Pierre. The body now lies in a funeral home somewhere in the city, exact location undisclosed.

As did the first, surprise number two hits us inside the headquarters of *la gendarmerie* shortly after four o'clock. We're seated in Colonel Tremblay's office, the door closed. The colonel sits behind his desk, Lieutenant Charpentier stands close by.

'The body will soon be transported to Newfoundland for burial, I assume.' I've steered us to communicating only in English. To save time and to be perfectly sure I have the facts straight.

'In time,' says the colonel.

My head jerks slightly, my bewilderment obvious.

'We have reason to suspect what you would call "foul play."'

Surprise number three madly crushes the first two.

'Foul play?' All three of us left staring into the eyes of the officer.

'Yes.' He hesitates. 'This is confidential, of course. Under investigation.'

He glances at an uncertain lieutenant, then turns back to us with penetrating seriousness.

'We discovered a lesion to his head, which may or may not be the result of an accidental fall against the rocks. But we also discovered what appears to be a knife wound to his right thigh.'

They what? 'Fuck.' Under my breath but unmistakeable.

No need to translate. The lieutenant coughs.

'The wound would not have killed him outright, but the loss of blood could certainly have contributed to his drowning.'

Nick shakes his head forcefully. Mae puts an arm around his shoulders.

The colonel turns to him. 'I understand you are also a student at the Francoforum.' He waits, allowing Nick time to recover. 'You and the deceased were friends?'

Nick manages to answer his questions, a couple of times switching to French when Lieutenant Charpentier looks particularly distant from the conversation.

The officers are especially interested in the previous episodes of cold-water swimming. As it turns out, Île aux Marins wasn't the only beach Nick and Zach had gone to.

'*La plage de Savoyard?*'

'*Oui.*'

Mae leans over and whispers, 'Not far from the *pointe du Diamant*, where we hiked. Remember the sign?'

I don't.

'*L'hypothermie, monsieur,*' says the lieutenant. '*C'était un souci, n'est-ce pas?*'

Nick reassures them both that no matter where they swam, they never showed signs of *l'hypothermie*. 'We were careful. If we got too cold, we came back to shore.'

'*La brigade de recherches* searched the shore in Île aux Marins,' the colonel says. 'They found no clothes, no shoes, no towel, no personal items of any kind.'

No glasses, no phone. Another revelation leaving us astounded.

Which can mean only one thing—someone grabbed it all and buggered off with it.

After stabbing him? I'm struggling to wrap my head around this.

I look over at Nick. Emotion overwhelms him again. He sinks into his chair.

Colonel Tremblay leans forward, his eyes on the young man. Then nods to the lieutenant, a sign that any further questions will wait.

Nevertheless, the police need a statement from each of us. The colonel makes clear what is to be included—full name, date of birth, temporary and permanent addresses, etc., followed by how we came to be on the beach in Île aux Marins, what we saw and did, etc., up to the point he and the officers arrived. Audio recordings will do, for now at least. We may each be asked later for additional information and to submit a signed written statement.

Another officer leads us to a small room, vacant except for a table and chairs. He leaves but is back again within a couple of minutes with recording equipment. Once it's set up, he demonstrates how to use it, then exits the room and closes the door.

We sit without speaking for a couple of minutes, collectively gathering the strength to get it over with.

Nick positions himself in front of the mic. But a potential problem looms.

'It's important that we're all on the same page,' I point out. 'Our stories need to line up.'

Nick and Mae look perplexed. As if it's not a foregone conclusion.

I clarify. 'We have to include the bit about the lifesaving crew.' '*Les Sauveteurs en Mer.*'

'What's your point?' Mae says.

A bit snappy there. It's been a long and very stressful day.

'My point is—what about Amélie calling the boyfriend?'

'Obviously that too.'

'And the video? She'll be in deep shit. I'm thinking it was an innocent gesture on her part. She thought she was being helpful. In her mind there was a chance Zach was still alive.'

'In her mind she was out to impress the boyfriend,' says Mae. 'You think we shouldn't say anything about it? Pretend we forgot it? Or worse yet, pretend it didn't happen?'

'I'm saying why not just leave it in her hands. Let Amélie be the one to tell the police.'

'Which I doubt she'll do. And if she does, don't you think the police will question why we said nothing about it? In which case we'll be the ones in shit. Really, Sebastian, think about it.'

My reaction to those choice few words I keep to myself.

I'm not stupid. Yes, I've thought about it. My investigative senses tell me Amélie knows more about what took place on that beach than she's letting on. I'm not sure what, but I'm betting there's something. And we have a better chance of finding out if we don't alienate the woman, which is just what will happen when she finds out we blew the whistle about the video.

Okay, so the PI in me is kicking in. Is that a surprise? No. A stab wound to the leg. Personal shit plundered. Weird fucking swim trunks. Yes, I've thought about it.

'Let's just get this done, okay?' says Nick, his stress level near the breaking point. 'Tell the *gendarmes* everything. Put it all in their hands. Let them friggin' handle it. They know what they're doing. They're the professionals.'

So what am I? Some amateur getting in the way?

I have all the sympathy in the world for Nick. He's going through a hell of a lot. But that hurt. Unintentionally, I'm sure.

In the meantime, we over-deliver. Drag the GoPro out in the open. Play super witness. In other effing words, demolish any hope I have of extracting vital, game-changing information from the potentially dodgy Amélie.

Enough unsaid. I capitulate.

We depart the room as one. Unsmiling, as expected. The trauma has hardly diminished.

Word reaches the colonel and he appears. 'Thank you. I realize this has not been easy. I suggest you try to get some rest. Your minds will be clearer in the morning.' He looks at Mae and me, in particular. 'In which case I suggest you both come by tomorrow. Shall we say eleven o'clock?'

'Sure.' We just want to have this over with.

'I must add that you are to remain in Saint-Pierre and Miquelon for the time being. The Investigative Unit may have additional questions.'

I wouldn't have expected otherwise. 'Fine.'

The colonel turns to Nick. 'Since you are a student here in Saint-Pierre, I know I can reach you anytime. I want you to understand, young man, that we are doing everything possible to find out how your friend died, and if in fact it is murder.'

We're stopped in our tracks, suddenly rewired. It's the first time the m-word has been uttered. It strikes Nick squarely in the face. For a second it threatens to crush him, but he holds it together. 'I understand,' he manages.

His faith in these policemen remains strong. I have to admit *la gendarmerie* radiates professionalism. Very efficient. Very French. *Liberté, Egalité, Fraternité* and all that. It is, after all, a total of twenty-seven *gendarmes* who have been dispatched from France to service a population of six thousand.

The odds are on their side. The case—for it is indeed now a case—may well be in exceptionally competent hands. Who am I to think otherwise?

However, what I do think (in fact, know) is that every police force, no matter how competent, could use a fresh perspective, especially if it comes with years of hard-fought experience in Newfoundland, where the deceased was born and raised and had his roots.

No point in being modest. It's suspected that my son's friend has been murdered. There's no way I'm about to sit on my ass, in anticipation that these dogged dudes in blue will have all the answers. No offence.

I lead the way out the door. The sudden waft of fresh air is more than welcome.

But then who should we see crossing the parking lot but Amélie Dubois, the person, I assume, next in line to take the attention of the colonel and his men. She's striding straight for the entrance.

'*Ça va?*' Serious in tone, but a deliberately informal choice on my part.

'*Pas si bien que ça,*' she replies.

Which, by the look on her face, I take to mean not so good. She's not prepared to linger. We are an unwelcome distraction. I smile and hold open the door.

She does add a few more words as she goes past me. '*Vous leur avez tout dit, je suppose.*'

Which goes over my head, but not Nick's. He answers her with a simple, '*Oui.*' She glares at me, not him.

I let the door close behind her. 'She's figured we told the whole truth,' says Nick.

'And nothing but the truth,' adds Mae, needlessly.

Later, in a quiet corner of Les P'tits Graviers, I'm hoping we can all recover, if only in part, from the day that has unfolded. Nick is still agitated, but enough time has passed that he is showing a turn for the better. Even so, he offers little interest in the menu.

'I'm having a burger and fries,' I tell him. 'Sounds very good.' Plain and unintimidating, something to fill a void without having to talk on about the more elaborate items of French cuisine on the menu. Nick hasn't eaten since breakfast. He needs something.

Mae sees where I am going with this. 'Me, too.'

I close the menu. 'Let's make it the three of us.' He doesn't say no.

While we're waiting, sipping Perrier, silence sets in. It's not what's needed.

'Did you guys notice that the ferry to Île aux Marins and this restaurant have the same name, one singular, one plural?'

'I did notice that,' says Mae. Not particularly natural in tone, but nevertheless purposeful. 'I'm not sure what it means.'

'Any idea, Nick?'

'Do you really want to know?' he says, edged with irritation.

Which Mae ignores. 'Absolutely,' she says. Better coming from her than me.

'*Les p'tits graviers*. The name for the boys who sailed over to work in the fishery. Hundreds of them. From Brittany and Normandy. They hauled the salt cod back and forth from the sheds to the stones and gravel to dry in the sun. Brutal work and they were paid next to nothing.'

Silence again for the moment. 'Very interesting.'

'Now I understand,' says Mae. 'I did know *gravier* meant gravel, but I didn't make the connection.'

Nick is hardly concerned one way or the other. He'd rather we talk ourselves, tune him out and let him deal with the messages on his phone. It looks like word has reached his classmates at the Francoforum.

It takes the burgers and fries to add some semblance of normalcy. Who can resist french fries when in France? They are superb. As are the hamburgers. What the generous slice of foie gras atop the beef patty does to the taste buds is wonderful.

My enthusiasm, however, remains unvoiced. Nick will be in no frame of mind to deal with it. He does consume a few fries and a small portion of the burger. He refuses my suggestion of wine, which I take to be in deference to his friend and their mutual fondness for it.

We forego dessert. We sip water and silently wonder how we'll bring the day to a close.

'Who?' Nick utters abruptly. Intense, if just audible. 'Who would want him dead?'

The foremost question. The next being, 'What can we do to help the police answer that?' A tactful way of posing it.

Nick looks at me. 'Your lack of French is a handicap.'

That may be somewhat true, but I have given that hurdle some thought and I'm confident I can clear it without any problem.

'You're forgetting my son speaks the language reasonably well and is getting better all the time.'

The penny takes a while to drop.

'I'm thinking about quitting. I won't be able to concentrate on my courses. Then there would be time . . .'

'No, man, don't quit.' It wasn't unexpected. 'It'll be hard, Nick, but I really think you should stick with it.'

He takes a deep breath.

'Zach would want you to. He'd want you to finish what you guys started.'

'Dad . . .'

'I know, I know. It'll be hell at times, but you'll have a lot of support from the rest of the class.'

He's unsure, emotion building again.

'There's another reason. It keeps you here in Saint-Pierre. It keeps you on top of whatever happens—the man in the field, if you want to put it that way. I'll need you if I'm going to get anywhere with an investigation.'

I had planned on avoiding that last word. Sounds so definite, like I know what I'm about at this point. Which I don't, exactly.

It derails his line of thought. 'I'm not sure you've worked out what you're getting yourself into. You've played ball with the RNC and the Mounties, but this is different. You're talking *la Gendarmerie nationale*. It's a whole different game.'

'I think what he means,' interrupts Mae, sensing my annoyance, 'is that psychologically this is different territory.'

That's a stopgap measure if I ever heard one.

She doesn't stop there. 'Remember that ball court we encountered when we were walking home last night? That high wall painted orange?'

Not easily forgotten. I nod, slightly. Convince me this is going somewhere useful.

'I looked it up. The wall is called a *fronton*. For a game brought over from the French Basque country.'

'*Pelote basque*,' mutters Nick.

'A very different ball game than what we're used to,' Mae adds. As if that makes any point whatsoever.

I look at one, then the other. 'So you're telling me that I'm not up for dealing with these *gendarmes*, that in other words I'm out of my friggin' league, to continue your analogy.'

I know, I know, it's inappropriate to the moment, in consideration of the heartbreak that has filled our day. But I can't help it. Where's their faith in me? Full stop. End of story.

They're silent. They realize they've struck a nerve. The damn ball is out of play.

It's not the note, however, on which our evening should end. 'I'm having dessert. I don't know about you guys.' I deliberately pick the item from the menu that looks the most difficult to pronounce. '*Pour moi . . . roulé à la fraise.*' It *roulés* off my tongue. Something to do with strawberries by the sound of it.

They play along, no doubt to placate me. Mae chooses *tarte aux pralines de Lyon*. Nick agrees to *mousse au chocolat*.

By the time I've paid the tab and we set ourselves in motion toward the exit, we're reasonably close to the relationship we've built over the years. We need each other. That goes without saying.

The time has come for Nick to make his way back to his boarding house. He hasn't said anything about it, but I expect the other students living there have been waiting for him to return. He needs to talk it through with others in his class.

We offer to walk with him, but he says no. With a quick 'Goodnight,' he breaks away. We watch as he slowly walks the length of the street to the intersection, then turns and is out of sight.

For his father and Mae, the night is also not yet over. Our minds need to settle if there's any hope of sleep. We undergo our nighttime rituals in preparation for bed, then don the white bathrobes. We install ourselves in armchairs, phones in hand, with the intention of finding out what else is going on in the world, not that it matters.

A glass of white wine is within Mae's reach. A dram of peaty Scotch within mine.

Both Nick and I have been back and forth with his mother. I text to update her one last time, then switch focus to Apple

News, quickly concluding I have no interest in the path of the latest hurricane. Nor does Mae, I'm sure.

I set the phone on the coffee table and focus on the Scotch. Mae glances at me. After a few minutes she also sets her phone aside. She holds the wine glass in her hand and soon takes a prolonged sip.

'I've been thinking,' she says. She takes another sip.

A good neutral start.

'There's something about Zach's swim trunks that needs investigation.'

I, of course, have been thinking the same thing, but just haven't had time to focus on it.

"Needs investigation" by whom is the towering question. Is this her way of saying she's had second thoughts about what part (if any) I might play in finding out why Zach met his end, i.e., what "*la* (overhyped) *Gendarmerie nationale*" has termed "foul play"?

'Curious you should say that.' I assume nothing.

'I saw you looking at Amélie's video. Were you able to see the trunks close up?'

As a matter of fact . . . 'Yes, I did.'

She waits for more. Which I deliver in increments, culminating with 'Icebergs aren't exactly well-suited to swimwear, in my opinion. Something's screwy.'

'In a colourway that's bright and tropical.'

"Colourway"—a new one on me. Then again, Mae owns a quilt shop.

'Does your store carry similar fabrics?'

'I've never seen anything like it, not from any of the suppliers I deal with. But of course it's out there somewhere. Someone designed it and had it made.' She pauses, staring at me. 'Doesn't it remind you of anything?'

'Vaguely.' I'm not sure what.

'That cap the kid in Rencontre East was wearing. The scrunchie the girl in Grand Bank had in her hair.'

A bit of a jolt, but after a moment, one that quickly dissipates. It doesn't add up. 'The guy was from Martinique. His designs were obviously tropical. He wasn't into codfish and icebergs.'

'He was on his way to Saint-Pierre, remember.'

'I don't get it. This guy somehow meets up with Zach and gives him a pair of trunks with a design that has no connection with Martinique, where the guy lives and, presumably, is what inspires his designs? It's not making sense to me.'

'Maybe he designed it especially for places like Saint-Pierre.'

'You mean for swimming in ice-cold water. Where swimming in the ocean is confined, no offence to Nick and Zach, to an eccentric few. Not exactly a big market potential.'

'Cold-water swimming has taken off across the northern hemisphere. It's exploding.'

More than a mild exaggeration. Let's put this in perspective. 'So before arriving on Saint-Pierre, fashion designer Philippe Jean creates a pattern using sea references specific to a cold climate but in a colourway that has nothing to do with this part of the world. Not only that, but he has the fabric made into trunks, which he brings with him. Here he finds a young man to wear them for what—a fashion shoot?'

It takes the wind out of her sails. Only momentarily. 'It's possible. I'm not saying it's entirely logical, but it is possible.'

'I grant you it's possible. But extremely far down the scale.'

'You're not thinking like a nineteen-year-old.'

Okay, so where is this about to land?

'Young adults deal in irony. They appreciate designs that are slightly crazed. Designs that say one thing but counter it with something else. So, codfish and icebergs with a tropical colour vibe. I can see it catching on anywhere where swimmers are all about cold water. They'd go crazy for it in Sweden and Norway.'

Really? The market potential has suddenly mushroomed to Scandinavia? I dare not say it, but—give me a break.

She has no trouble sensing my persistent skepticism. 'You might be right.' While being careful not to alienate me yet again.

We return to our phones. The hurricane story might not be so tiresome after all.

Just when I reach the point of thinking I'll call it a night, having some confidence that I'll fall asleep, Mae perks up.

She doesn't say anything, just reaches across and hands me her phone. I'm expected to see something that will interest me. Not the path of the hurricane eventually reaching Newfoundland, I would hope.

Originating in the Caribbean, but, no, not the hurricane. Quite far from it.

Some guy up to his knees in frozen slushy water, snow-capped mountains in the background. Wearing trunks full of crabs, lobsters, seals, whales, and codfish, and icebergs. Intertwined in a tropical colourway. I'll be goddamned.

'I searched cold-water swimming sites on Instagram. Posted two days ago. Not by Philippe Jean. By some guy called Axel in a place called Tromsø.'

'Where's that?'

'Norway.' She takes a moment to let it sink in before adding. 'Axel gets around apparently. Looks like he has a passion and a bucket list of countries. Just scroll down.'

That would be Axel in . . . Sweden . . . Finland . . . Iceland (appropriately enough) . . . Good God. I stop scrolling at Murmansk, Russia. 'I notice it's only in this last posting that he's wearing those particular trunks.'

'A recent purchase, we can only assume.'

'Possibly.' That's as far as I'll go.

'Want me to message him and ask?'

There's no solid reason to say no. The time difference puts Axel in the middle of the night in Norway. *If* he answers it won't be for several hours. After another ball-freezing swim probably.

While Mae messages, I discard my robe and make for the bed. Dressed only in a fresh pair of Manmade boxers. I discard the decorative pillows and sink between the sheets.

I'm still awake when Mae joins me. There's a longish period when we both pretend we're trying hard to fall asleep. We have a lot still on our minds.

A few minutes later, unexpectedly, a hand comes to rest just above my hip. Lingers there, but only for a moment. The fingers press in and under the waistband. Her hand is bloody cold. If I didn't know better I'd say she's soaked it in ice water before coming to bed. The hand suddenly encases what lies below. I flinch. 'Fuck.'

'It's not unlike cold-water swimming,' she says.

CINQ

'AXEL ANSWERED. AWESOME.'

The words jerk me awake. Not what a fellow wants or needs, given that my blurry eyes detect no evidence of daylight. Couldn't she have put her phone on silent mode for the night? Like we all do.

She just couldn't wait to find out where her guesswork has led.

I try sitting up in bed, with limited success. Mae reaches over the side and hands me a selection of decorative pillows to stuff behind my back and head. So, they do have a practical use. That's reassuring, except they angle me uncomfortably.

'Ready?' The pre-dawn excitement in her voice has only increased.

It takes more shifting about but, yes, I am now game to hear what Axel has on his mind. 'Fire away.' Let the Norwegian saga begin.

–*Thank you for your note. Yes, I do think they look good on me. A very nice contrast to the pans of ice. I purchased them in Oslo last week. I can send you the address if you like. You might not be in luck. They are selling out fast. Or as I like to say—selling like* aebleskivers. *By the way I am saving up to come to Canada. I plan to swim above the Arctic Circle in all 8 countries it cuts through. I think it could get me in the Guinness Book of World Records. Wish me luck!*

Well, isn't that a boost to the prospect of getting out of bed and facing the day. Mae doesn't gloat. Which is good.

'What the hell are *aebleskivers*?' To shift attention away from having to eat crow.

'Why don't I google that?'

In the meantime, I'll just readjust the decorative pillows. Not for long. Google quickly delivers. And there they are—*aebleskivers*, Norwegian pancakes. In other words, hotcakes. I should have known. Except these are filled.

'With lingonberries,' Mae declares, having read the fine print. Her level of excitement just jumped another notch. 'What we call partridgberries. How cool is that?'

Way cool. And with that our day outside the interesting confines of the bed begins.

At breakfast, which doesn't include hotcakes of any description, I'm ready to lay out plans to make the best use of our remaining time in Saint-Pierre. There's the option of me staying on and Mae flying back to St. John's to meet her work commitments, but that depends on what other investigative leads we prod to the surface over the next twenty-four hours.

Before we get into the details of where to start, I get a text from Nick.

–I'll give it a try

Yes. I'd say that talking with the other students helped to change his mind.

I have to be careful how I word my reply. I can't be cheering him on like the father in me is desperate to do. Keep it adult to adult, letting him work it through on his own terms.

–I think you've made a good decision.

–See how it goes

–Mae and I will check in with you after classes.

–OK

"See how it goes" is also on the plus side. Keeping in mind he's going through hell.

I show Mae the screen. She agrees—all eyes on the positive.

Back to the investigative details. 'I say we start by filling in the *gendarmes* on the business of the swim trunks. Let's see where they're willing to take it.'

Our optimism leads us to arrive early. Only to find that Tremblay is not in his office, resulting in an unscheduled meeting with a hyper Lieutenant Charpentier.

It looks to me like the officer is struggling to cope with the pressure of keeping his investigation moving ahead at a serious pace. Now complicated by the sudden face-to-face with us, language barrier included.

Picture this: Mae has her phone rather close to his face, with the image of Axel in Murmansk in his trunks surrounded by ice pans. Which she is using to establish the connection to Zach and *his* trunks in Île aux Marins.

The lieutenant fails to make the cognitive leap. At which point we attempt to bring Philippe Jean into the picture.

'*Martinique?*' says the lieutenant, something having been triggered somewhere in his head. '*Ah, Martinique. Le soleil. Les plages.*'

We were hoping for more. Mae's earnest, if limited, French has lost its usefulness. My swimming motions in combination with pauses to shiver profusely only confuse the message.

Charpentier points to his watch. To speed things along he calls in another officer whose understanding of English is better than his own.

Unfortunately, not by much. It is barely enough to clarify matters to the point that we now think Lieutenant Charpentier understands that Philippe Jean, the designer of the trunks, was likely in Saint-Pierre, or in fact may still be here.

The lieutenant opens his notebook to a blank page and makes an entry. I am not impressed by its length. I get the feeling the few words he's scrawled are an attempt to get us out of his hair.

'*Merci*,' he says. '*Merci de m'avoir signalé ce fait*.'

The other officer translates. In other words, thanks for this. Subtext: I have a helluva lot more than swimming trunks needing my attention.

Disgruntled, but at least making an attempt not to show it, I initiate an exit. Mae puts away her phone and follows. '*Merci*,' she says in passing. It edged toward the curt, which needs no translation.

Then, coming through the front entrance, just as we're heading toward it, is Colonel Tremblay. There's still hope. He invites us into his office.

'You showed up early. But I see you've met with Lieutenant Charpentier. He'll bring me up to date. I was at the funeral home finalizing the travel arrangements for the autopsy.'

Which gives me more hope. It appears the local hospital doesn't do autopsies, so the body would have to be transported to the nearest one that does, which would be St. John's. Where I'll be in a couple of days and where I have, shall we say, an in with the pathology lab.

'In the summer we have a direct flight to Paris, but in this case we'll have to connect through Montreal.'

I'm struck dumb, then amused. The man is having us on. Mae's not so sure. 'You mean the body has to be flown all the way to Paris?'

'We're in France, *madame*.' In a tone that confirms there is no humour in play.

'A long flight,' is all I manage. I'm tempted to mention to

the colonel that an autopsy is best performed within twenty-four hours of death, before the body starts to decompose. I refrain, unwilling to risk the solid relationship we've had up to this point.

Mae is less guarded. 'Even if the body is that of a Canadian citizen?'

'We are in contact with the Canadian Embassy in Paris, *madame*. In due course the body will be turned over to them for transportation to Canada and to the next-of-kin.'

Who live in Lamaline, which is a stone's throw across the water from Saint-Pierre and a four-hour drive from St. John's.

'Two long flights.' Again my tongue is curbed. Overriding the insertion of the word "unnecessary."

Time to change subjects to what one hopes is a more logical display of police logistics. Namely, the business of the swim trunks. Rather than leave it in the hands of Lieutenant Charpentier to convey, and risk the key points being lost in translation, I quickly relate what has been discovered, concluding with the observation that the connection with Philippe Jean, in our view, needs to be investigated.

'Martinique,' notes the colonel. 'Interesting.'

His "interesting" exudes disinterest.

'Lieutenant Charpentier and I will discuss it,' he tells us. 'We'll get back to you. I will say that at this point codfish and icebergs on the swimming trunks would be less of a focus than the stab wound.'

Meaning no focus whatsoever.

The colonel sees fit to add, 'You realize, of course, that icebergs are rarely seen in the waters off Saint-Pierre and Miquelon. We are not on the route.'

Technically true, but entirely irrelevant. I remain outwardly calm enough to point out, 'Icebergs are a universal symbol of cold water and therefore cold-water swimming.'

'And since the cod moratorium in 1992, the value of codfish to our economy has been surpassed by other exports. The orange-footed sea cucumber is a very important species at the moment.'

Orange-footed bloody sea cucumber? You want that on a pair of trunks? It's a warty log. Sure to be a hit, *n'est-ce* fucking *pas?* Pardon my French.

A solid but inconspicuous breath. My irritation is in hand. My blood pressure is under control. I'm verging on being both outwardly and inwardly calm.

Mae reaches out and touches my arm. 'We should be going. We don't want to be taking up any more of the colonel's time. Thank you, sir. We'll be in touch, I'm sure.'

The colonel is smiling. Cool as a bloody orange-footed sea cucumber.

We escape the confines of *la gendarmerie*. We seat ourselves on a bench in *Square Joffre*, sipping cappuccinos from paper cups, and making the most of the two pastries also purchased by Mae from a nearby café. A little *pause café*, she calls it.

She knows I'm a sucker for *millefeuille*. Sinful, messy, decadent. It comes close to taking my mind off what recently transpired. Not close enough.

'They have a lot coming at them,' Mae offers.

Her line catches me mid-mouthful. 'More than they can handle,' I mutter. I make short work of what's left of the pastry and down the remainder of the cappuccino.

The path is clear for a course correction in the investigation. What was a generous offer of assistance to the self-centred *brigade de recherches* has shrunk to an alien PI and his partner going at it alone.

'They had their chance.'

Let's see if they will be, in due course, *très* contrite. Let them eat sea cucumber, to take a cue from a certain queen of France.

'This really got to you.'

'I'm ready to move on.' The vitriol has run its course. 'So, how do we track down *Monsieur* Philippe Jean?'

A smile surfaces. 'I think you actually prefer it this way. You like running your own show. Pumped to do one better than the police.'

I return the smile. She's not looking for a response, but I have one anyway.

'This is how I see it at this point. If Philippe Jean is the designer behind the trunks, then there's a good chance he's approached a local upscale clothing shop to see if it would be interested in carrying his product. Am I right?'

'Sounds logical.'

Logical is good. 'As soon as you finish up, we're on our way.'

She's somewhat invigorated, I can tell. Somewhat invigorated is also good.

'Where shall we start?'

The fact is we don't know the locations of such shops. Walking around blindly, hoping to strike one, seems a waste of time.

'I suspect,' says Mae, 'you're not going to find what you have in mind. I'm willing to bet that guys with the euros to spend on high-end clothes do their shopping in Montreal . . . or Paris.'

'I doubt it. Maybe some, but not all.'

We're at an impasse. A cul-de-sac. A little competition is healthy in a relationship.

'In that case we need informed local input,' she says. 'How about we put it in the hands of tourist information?'

Mae leads the way to the office, located opposite the *place du Général de Gaulle.* She strides up to the nicely dressed young man behind the desk whose job I'm sure doesn't pay him enough that he can dash off to Montreal to buy designer gear. Let alone Paris.

He responds without reservation. He produces a street map and circles three different locations, writing the name of each shop in the margins of the map. He is leery of ranking them. Favouritism by the tourist office would not sit well with shops two and three.

I'm delighted with his help. 'Thank you, *monsieur*, you've been most generous. By the way, that's a very good-looking shirt you're wearing.'

We sit on the bench outside the office and blindly weigh the merits of each location. I could suggest checking online reviews, but I don't put much stock in them. When possible I like getting my own hands on the merchandise.

'Impromptu,' Mae announces decisively. Her enthusiasm overshadows any need to concede defeat. 'Impromptu. Something unexpected. It speaks to me.'

And so it should. 'We're off then. I'm excited.'

I'm not being facetious. And for good reason. Impromptu turns out to be exactly what I had in mind.

The boutique carries mostly women's clothes (no surprise), but the men's section is looking upscale and promising. I discreetly check the labels.

'Look at this.' For a breath-stopping moment, I thought the label said Martinique.

'*Matínique*.' Mae pronounces it with flair. 'This would look good on you.'

I check the price tag. 'Not in the foreseeable future.'

'How about these?'

She's pointing to a rack of underwear. Brand name on the waistband: Pullin. Never heard of it. She looks through the rack and withdraws a pair. Bright blue, green, and orange. Tropical vegetation interlaced with several tiger heads, one of which has its canines bared, noticeably positioned at the crotch. Feral *risqué* you might say.

'It's your style.'

A rather provocative observation there, Mae. The boxers might be designed to arouse the tiger in me, but they're redundant, my love, especially at that price.

'*Bonjour. Comment puis-je vous aider?*'

A welcome interruption. The owner of the shop, I presume. She's about our age, but in keeping with the ambience, looking much more trendy.

'*Merci, madame,*' answers Mae. '*Nous avons une question.*'

Yes, we do in fact have a number of them. Which I hope can be revealed in my first (and generally, only) language. I test the waters. 'Yes, *madame*, if you would be so kind.'

'I will do my best.' She is a little hesitant, but I suspect she gets considerable practice with the tourists who venture into her boutique.

'Would the name Philippe Jean mean anything to you? He's a fashion designer. From Martinique.'

It catches her off guard. She's of course unsure where this is leading. She answers with a tentative 'Yes.'

'Among other things, he designs men's swimwear.'

'Yes.'

Mae and I glance at each other as the woman leaves us for what we presume is a back room.

She reappears, with something in her hand.

'Well, shit,' I utter beneath my breath while staring intently at what she is holding.

She's holding a duplicate pair of the now infamous codfish/iceberg swimming shorts.

'He was here, in your shop?'

'He left me these, together with some other items.'

'For consideration as a line you would carry?' asks Mae.

'Yes. *Exactement.*'

'So not to sell as yet?'

'No, no, just to consider.'

'What do you think? Do you like the design?'

'For swimming in cold water, yes. Our water is very cold. His design is, how do you say, *approprié.*'

'Appropriate,' says Mae.

'Apropos,' I insert.

'*Oui, à propos.*'

Nice. 'And what did you think of Philippe Jean? I mean as a person?'

The shop owner is perplexed.

'His personality. Did he seem sincere?'

'*Oui.* Charming man. Yes.'

'And when was he here, in the shop?'

She's thinking. 'Last week. Friday. He had just come from *la plage de Savoyard.*'

Really? That same beach where Nick and Zach had gone to swim.

'He was very excited. He loved *les couleurs.*'

'The colours?'

So what's with that?

'The colours of . . . the . . . *la clôture.*'

Mae is struggling. As am I. 'The culture? The culture of cold-water swimming?'

Mae whispers to me, 'That doesn't make sense.' In her opinion.

The shop owner tries again, '*La barrière.*'

'The barrier?' says Mae. And how much sense does that make?

'Yes, the *barrière.*'

I'm not convinced. Nevertheless, we can't get bogged down in translation. Something is colourful, we know that much.

'We'll check it out,' says Mae, aside to me, then turning back to the shop owner, '*Merci, madame.*'

Madame does have a bit more to offer. Eagerly this time. She is certain Philippe Jean has left Saint-Pierre. 'Yesterday he was flying to *Montréal*, and then home. That's what he told me.'

'*Merci, madame*. You have been very helpful.'

'Tell me, please—why are you interested in this man?'

Of course I should have anticipated the question. It makes for some quick thinking.

'Fabric, madame. We are into fabric.' I glance at Mae.

She picks up on the hint. 'Yes, we are . . . I am. I have a fabric shop in St. John's.'

'We saw a picture of the fabric online,' I tell her. 'It caught our eye. The codfish, of course, being from Newfoundland. And the icebergs.'

'That is a surprise. I did not think he was ready to show it yet.'

'Just to a Norwegian friend. I think he was looking for market reaction before he goes into full production. He's testing the waters, so to speak.' I'm chuckling.

It doesn't translate well. It leads the woman back to being perplexed.

In the meantime, quick-thinking Mae heads to the men's wear section of the store. A move to draw attention away from the shop owner's confusion. She quickly rejoins us.

A move also to placate her. In Mae's hand is a pair of the formidable tiger briefs. 'I'll take these,' she says. 'A little gift for *monsieur*.' She glances cheekily at me, then leads the way to the checkout counter, where Mae shares with the owner a brief but knowing smile.

'Oh, you women.'

It secures the change in focus. I insert a manly smile, paired with a low-pitched, tigerish growl. Mae and I head promptly for the door.

On the sidewalk outside Impromptu, we're feeling pleased with ourselves. The teamwork paid off nicely.

Next stop—the something "colourful" at *la plage de Savoyard.* It's a slog I remind her, roughly the same distance as the relentless *pointe du Diamant* trek. 'A taxi is the better choice.'

'Not better health-wise.'

How about the more logical choice? Not that it's going to do us any good to get caught up in semantics.

'But maybe better time-wise.' She's come around.

Teamwork somewhat intact, it's not long before we're standing together on *la plage de Savoyard*, the taxi driver on standby in the parking lot. It's reinvigorating to discover just what's so colourful.

Savoyard is actually a lake, barely inland from the ocean that surrounds the *pointe du Diamant*. According to Mae (who it seems made very good use of her time in the taxi) five hundred tons of sand were brought in to make the beach a prime summer attraction for the *Saint-Pierrais*. As for the "colourful," a long, semicircular fence of upright posts separates the sandy beach from the grassy picnic area behind it, wooden posts of varying heights clamped tight together and painted bright pastels—green, blue, orange, yellow, and purple.

'I would call that mauve,' says Mae when we have finally grasped the whole of it. 'I'm also thinking tropical hibiscus,' she adds.

Right on. She's thinking not only tropical hibiscus. Like me, she's friggin' thinking tropical Philippe Jean. Except for the water temperature and lack of palm trees, this beach could be in bloody Martinique. 'Make no friggin' wonder the guy was excited.' In his mind it outright confirmed the palette he picked for his cold-water swimwear.

Putting aside whatever possessed the city council of Saint-Pierre to opt for such incongruous colours, this is a revelation.

Swimming is swimming. Cold water. Warm water. Saint-Pierre. Martinique. It's total immersion. There is something altogether hedonistic about enveloping your flesh in liquid and thrusting through it. Letting every last fraction of skin be blessedly coated. The beast of a man wrapt in the cosmos. Nude, perfectly nude, by choice. If not, then in a perfectly hedonistic pair of trunks.

I finally come up for air. Mae is staring at me, wondering where the heck my mind has gone. It's gone to places best kept to myself.

'What do you think, Mae? Do you think *Monsieur* Philippe came away thinking, "yes, love for tropical colours is universal"? In fact, everyone loves their exuberance, their optimism, their *joie de vivre*. Thinking, "yes, these trunks of mine will sell anywhere."'

'I believe you're right. Philippe Jean left here wondering how he could use this spot to market his merchandise.'

I hadn't thought that far ahead. I catch up quickly. 'You mean like a photo shoot?'

'It must have been in his mind. It was too good an opportunity to pass up.'

'He only had a couple of days. I'm not sure he had time enough to pull that off. For one thing, where would he get a model?'

The taxi takes us straight back to Impromptu.

'You've returned. And so soon,' madame says as we enter her shop. 'No refund on underwear, I'm sorry.' She's kidding us, I'm sure.

'We have a couple more questions. If you don't mind.'

'About Philippe Jean?' She's not surprised.

'Did he ever mention anything about a photo shoot on Saint-Pierre? By chance, did he mention anything about needing a model?'

She is surprised by the directness of the questions. A hesitant '*Oui.*'

I'm feeling an investigative jolt. Yet she needs a prompt for the details.

'Did he find someone?' says Mae.

The shop owner is looking increasingly uncomfortable. 'I'm not sure.'

She may not be sure, but only because there's something she's not telling us. 'You think maybe he did?' I ask, the urgency turned up a notch. 'Perhaps you suggested someone?'

A longish pause. '*Oui.*'

'Do you mind telling us who?' Mae says, switching to a more gentle approach.

She slowly retrieves her phone. She nervously scrolls though several screens before stopping. 'He came in the store last week. He tried on this Matínique shirt. He didn't buy it. He was a student, he couldn't afford it. But it looked very good on him. I asked if I could take a picture for our Facebook page. I would pay him. Not much, but something. He agreed.' She pauses. 'I took down the page. After I heard the rumours.' She passes us the phone.

It's hardly a surprise.

But it is a shock seeing the young man looking so alive and well.

'Zach Russell.'

She is more unsettled than ever. I quickly explain, 'He was a friend of my son. They were students together at the Francoforum.'

'Then it is true?'

As far as I know the police haven't yet released his name. But it's found a way into the community nonetheless. I see no reason not to confirm it.

'That is why you are asking about Philippe Jean. You must think there is a connection.'

Now she's the one applying pressure. I strain to find a way around it. 'No connection. Not now. Just questions.' Vague, and not enough to satisfy her.

Mae steps in. 'Madame, if Philippe Jean did set up a photo shoot with Zach Russell, do you have any idea where it might have been staged?'

It calms the waters, somewhat.

'If he wanted him on a beach, there are two to choose from. I think you know both of them.'

Her patience is running thin. I think it best if we ease ourselves out of the conversation. At least for now. There is always the option of returning to the boutique if we need to.

'Goodbye and thank you, madame. Would you mind telling us your name?'

There's a pause. She must realize we would find out, if not from her then from another source. 'My name is Monique.'

'Mae.' She holds out her hand. '*Merci.*' They shake hands briefly. Mae passes her a business card. 'If you're ever in St. John's, please come by my shop. We have an interesting inventory of fabrics.'

I follow with, '*Sébastien.*'

'*Sébastien.*'

I suspect a handshake would be out of place.

'I think there's a lot more Monique could have told us,' I say to Mae as we take our seats at Café Solidaire.

'I'm not so sure. What reason would she have to protect Philippe Jean? And if she did have a reason, it's not likely she would have told us as much as she did.'

Good point. Well . . . okay. Refocus, reboot.

Leaving us with a need for other sources to broaden our picture of the man. 'Our priority now is finding more people he had contact with while in Saint-Pierre. For starters, where was he staying?'

He had plenty of choices—hotels, *auberges*, B & Bs, Airbnb, VRBO—so many that the task of contacting them all seems daunting. Not to mention time-consuming. 'Is there a way to narrow it down to what we think would be most likely?'

'Based on?'

'What he might be looking for in accommodation, given what we know of him.'

'Which I'm afraid is not a great deal at this point.'

Let's keep it positive, Mae. 'He's artistic for one thing, so he'd be looking for something out of the ordinary, a place with character. He likes meeting local people, chatting with them, finding out more about the place he's visiting, all of which I would say rules out hotels.'

In the meantime the server has arrived, ready to take our lunch order. We've yet to look at the menu board.

'*Avez-vous une recommandation, s'il vous plaît?*' Mae asks.

Which speeds things up. She goes with the *tarte oignons, blettes, jambon*. Ditto for me. Not sure what *blettes* will turn out to be but they sound promising. With a side of *verrine de betteraves et Chantilly ciboulette*. Haven't got a clue.

The server heads for the kitchen. We're back to the matter of our man from Martinique and his most likely accommodation. While Mae was ordering, the thought occurred to me that Pascal at our *auberge* could be of help. I drop him a text.

–Bonjour, Pascal. We've discovered that someone we know of from Martinique has been staying in Saint-Pierre. Wondering if you might have a suggestion of what accommodation he might choose. He's a fashion designer who likes to chat. A bit offbeat.

I show it to Mae before sending it off.

'I wonder if there's a chance . . .' she says.

Ding. That was quick.

–Philippe Jean?

I turn the screen toward her. 'How the hell did he know that?'

–yes

Ding.

–Here. He checked out at 1 yesterday. I dropped him at the airport.

It takes a moment to register.

'He stayed at Auberge Daguerre?' Mae prods.

'I'll be damned. And we didn't run into him, even at breakfast.'

'Breakfast started at 7:30. We never got there before 8:30.'

True enough. And we were long gone by the time he checked out.

One last text to Pascal.

–We have questions.

–no problem

–Be there soon.

Blettes turn out to be chard, which is a non-event, at least for me. But luckily the other ingredients outdo themselves. The tart is a winner. I had my eye on *gâteau aux carottes* for dessert, but for the sake of time, we forego it and coffee.

It takes less than ten minutes to get to the *auberge*. Pascal is behind the reception desk and, as always, ready to be helpful to guests. Whether that includes sharing information about other guests remains to be seen. Let's greet him with a generous smile and assume that under certain circumstances he will.

A preamble is necessary. He knows about the death on Île aux Marins, of course, and the fact that the police are involved. What he doesn't know is that we are the ones who, together with Nick, discovered the body. Nor, obviously, is he aware that the deceased was wearing swim trunks designed by Philippe Jean.

The clincher of the intrigue is only a few words away. I lower my voice. 'Don't breathe a word . . . but foul play is suspected.'

He's speechless.

'Mae and I have spent a considerable amount of time with *la gendarmerie* since it all happened.'

Now for the transition.

'Lieutenant Charpentier says to say hello by the way. You'll be interested to know he's given me a role in the investigation. You see, Pascal, I am what you call a *détective privé*.' I'm thinking it will sink in more seamlessly in French.

'It's your occupation?'

'*Oui*.' (Well, part-time, but there's no point in getting into that.) 'So, to make a long story short, the police are letting me handle the connection to Philippe Jean. As you can imagine, they are a bit overwhelmed at the moment.'

'I see.'

And what I see is the need to rework the scenario a little more to up his comfort level. 'I've been at this for a number of years. And, of course, I'm fully certified. I've been involved in a number of high-profile cases in Newfoundland. You might not have heard about them, living as you do in Saint-Pierre.'

He hasn't. Which is a good thing.

So let's just plunge right in. 'We've discovered that the boutique Impromptu is planning to carry his swim trunks, the same design as the pair worn by the deceased. What I'm wondering is whether, when you two spoke to each other, if he ever mentioned he was arranging to have someone model them, in a photo shoot perhaps?'

A strange and somewhat delicate question, it appears. Pascal hesitates, he struggles to answer and his face turns slightly red.

'Did he ask *you*, by chance?' Mae says. My eyes flicker. It's a surprise to think it even crossed her mind.

'I declined. Not in keeping with my image as the owner of an *auberge*. Plus it was too damn cold.'

Really? I would have thought Pascal was a bit old for that gig. Obviously Philippe Jean was aiming to expand the market potential of his swimwear.

That, or he had other, shall we say, provocative things in mind and this was testing the waters.

'But he did find *someone*,' Mae says. 'He found a young man by the name of Zach Russell—the deceased.'

Pascal takes a moment, wondering perhaps what might have happened to him if he had been the one to don the swimwear. 'It is not a name that came up in our conversations.'

'What names did?' I ask.

'Only one as I recall.' There's a brief pause. 'Johnny Smith.'

Rather unremarkable. And obviously not French.

'Someone came up to him at the bar in Le Rustique the evening before. He was wondering if I knew anything about a guy named Johnny Smith.'

'Someone interested in modelling for him?'

'He didn't say. And I didn't ask. I know a lot of people in Saint-Pierre, but there's a lot I don't know. With a name like that he wasn't from here. Maybe he's another student at the Francoforum.'

'Possibly.' There's an easy way to find out.

Beyond this, there's not much more of investigative interest in what Pascal has to tell us. He and Philippe Jean had a number of chats during his stay, but they didn't amount to much more than the guy singing the praises of the beaches in Martinique.

'You should book a flight,' I tell Pascal. 'Cold water would no longer be an excuse for you not to model his swimwear.'

He only chuckles. Maybe feeling it's good to be alive.

Next destination—the Francoforum. Nick's classes end at 2:50. We arrive at 2:45 to find him seated in the otherwise empty foyer. He's looking like he's had a rough day.

'Hey, pal, how's it's goin'?' As upbeat as I can make it without sounding obtuse.

'Not great.'

I sit next to him. Mae wanders away, as if attracted to the various bulletin boards.

'I had to leave class early. I couldn't handle it.'

'It'll get easier.'

'I'm not so sure.'

I rest a hand of top of his. 'Life is the shits. You hope it gets better and it will. It's bound to take time. Give yourself some time.'

The class has ended and other students wander into the foyer. When I see them heading our way I stand up and walk toward Mae. They gather around Nick. Their demeanour is quiet, unassuming. I can't hear them, but I can only think they're offering words of encouragement.

Obviously it's no secret the feelings Nick had for Zach. I'm curious if Zach's ran as deep for Nick. We might never know.

The person in charge of MUN's immersion program arrives. I recognize her from some group pictures Nick has sent me. When she's not in Saint-Pierre, she's back home in St. John's, teaching at the university. Her name is Sasha. We introduce ourselves.

'I thought of cancelling classes, but I felt it important that they all come together and support each other. Some of them have taken it very hard, Nick in particular.'

'Zach was his best friend here.' I don't go beyond that. I'm sure she has her own perspective.

'I arranged for a trauma counsellor. He spoke only French, and in some cases I had to translate, so it was not ideal, but it was helpful. A couple of the other students have lost friends or family in recent years, and they were very good at generating discussion.'

'They need a path forward,' Mae says.

'We're all devastated.' The emotion overtakes her for the moment, but she continues. 'It'll take time and, as I said to the students, the best thing we can do for Zach is to find our way back to the program and complete what we came to Saint-Pierre to do.'

'Nick was wanting to quit but I've been trying to get him past that.'

Mae adds, 'He doesn't realize it, but it would be harder if he did quit. He'd be totally preoccupied with what happened. There'd be so much more strain on his mental health.'

We all quietly agree. We seem to have reached the point where I can turn to another matter.

'Sasha, would you happen to have heard of someone by the name of Johnny Smith? We think he might have recently crossed paths with Zach. We're wondering if he is or was a student at the Francoforum.'

It only takes a second. 'Not now certainly, and it's not a name I recall from all the years I've been here. Other universities conduct immersion programs at the Francoforum—Dalhousie, for example—although we're the only group here at the moment.'

That ends that speculation. I have other questions.

'I assume the *gendarmerie* has been in touch? I assume they'll want to talk to the students as part of their investigation.'

'There are officers coming in at ten tomorrow morning.'

I would love to be a fly on the wall. But of course, when I think about it, I'll come very close to being just that. I glance over at Nick. He'll be my eyewitness to the session with the *brigade de recherches*, Clément Charpentier in the lead.

Not to pre-empt the good lieutenant, but I pass along the fact that the body is en route to Paris. I see no reason the police should be keeping it a secret. It'll be less of a shock coming from her than being sprung on the students by the lieutenant.

She shows no surprise. She's spent enough time in Saint-Pierre to have heard of another instance where an autopsy was needed. 'It's what happens,' she says. 'In this case, because of the stab wound . . .' Upset, but not surprised.

So she knows the unfortunate detail. It could only have come from Nick. That's fine. He's dealing with the reality of what happened.

'Thanks, Sasha. It's been a rough couple of days.' Mae is more demonstrative. She gives Sasha a hug. I am always amazed how women bond so quickly in these situations.

I lead the way back to Nick. Since the other students appeared he's become increasingly talkative, a positive scenario that I don't want to interrupt. I quickly let him know that we'll check in with him later. It's better if he goes back to his boarding house and has supper there. Another step back to a routine.

Neither Mae nor I are particularly hungry. We have too much on our minds. Instead of a restaurant meal, we decide to look into what's on offer at the Super U. The supermarket is a short walk from the Francoforum.

Among several choices at its deli is freshly prepared *tartiflette*. Looks promising.

Mae has had it before, 'In the Haute-Savoie, when I was in my twenties, skiing in the Alps.'

Really, skiing in the Alps? While I was freezing my butt off ice fishing on a pond in the backwoods of Newfoundland, chowing down a can of Vienna sausages and sucking on a thermos of tea, Mae was carving up the powder in the French

Alps, followed, *après ski*, by wine and *tartiflette*. Impressive. You learn something new about your partner every day.

'Potatoes, bacon, onion, cream, and reblochon cheese—just five ingredients. But you know the French—they can do amazing things with five ingredients.'

I have no doubt. Not that I've ever heard of Reblochon.

While Mae waits at the counter for two portions of amazing *tartiflette* to be boxed, I head for the wine section to pick up a *demi-bouteille* (a word I picked up while ski-less in France).

I'm sidetracked en route. Adjacent to the tiers of wine is a substantial spirits section. Zach flashes across my mind, and our conversation about whisky two evenings ago.

And here it is before me—*Eddu*. The whisky Zach had thought about buying.

Eddu Brocéliande. Distillerie des Menhirs. Produit de Bretagne. A blended whisky, made using buckwheat.

Mae is now looking over my shoulder at the box I'm holding in my hand. 'You need to buy it.'

How good it would have been to share a dram with the young man and my son. And how disheartening a thought is that. Still, I can't not buy the whisky. It would almost be disparaging his memory.

While we're at the checkout, Mae asks the cashier for directions to a green space where we can sit and eat. *Étang Boulot*, just across the street, she tells us.

The small lake is circled by a pathway that appears to be free of walkers at this hour of the day. We stop at the first park bench we come to, open our respective portions of *tartiflette* and fill two small paper cups with a lively Riesling from Alsace. The wine pairs well with the nutty aftertaste of the cheese, which hits the taste buds with rustic charm. No ski lodge with blazing fireplace, but if one ignores the major boulevard running past it, *Étang Boulot*, too, has a certain pastoral pull on the senses.

'You can't fool me,' says Mae, glancing at the empty box in my lap. 'You loved it.' The fact that my serving has been consumed long before hers would seem to confirm her observation. She laughs, 'You just like playing hard to get.'

Can't help but love the woman. Anyone who can combine sexual innuendo with *tartiflette* wins my vote.

It's been a while since we broke out laughing together. Which is not like us. The tension of the last couple of days has been hard going. We needed that release.

We needed it, but it's destined to be short-lived. Besides the worry of Nick, there's the pressure of making the best use of the time we have remaining in Saint-Pierre.

We head back to the *auberge*. Mae needs a while, for want of better words, "to freshen up." As compared to me who sits and removes the bottle of *Eddu* whisky from its box and examines it more closely.

Nick had agreed to meet at seven at Le Rustique. The exchange of texts was cut and dried, no indication of his state of mind at the moment. We hope for the best, and brace ourselves for the possibility that he has sunk again into despair.

In the meantime, Johnny Smith is up for discussion. Mae has googled Canada 411 and found that the search for "J Smith" coughs up eighty-nine matches, assuming he lives in Newfoundland. And has a landline.

'Which I doubt,' she says. 'Ten to one all he uses is a cell.'

We quickly reach the conclusion that it's not worth the effort it would take to contact everyone on the list on the slim chance we would strike someone who was recently in Saint-Pierre, let alone was willing to admit it and to encountering one Philippe Jean.

Our hope now is that a bartender at Le Rustique remembers him.

We arrive early to pose the question. Standing at the bar, I order a *Miqu'Ale*, an IPA from a local craft brewery.

'Hoppy and a bit bitter. Very good,' I say to the young woman behind the bar who poured it.

Mae follows suit, choosing their *Pilsner des Mers*. '*Grande fraîcheur en bouche.*'

'*Oui, oui. Je l'aime aussi.*'

Now that my credit card has dealt with the total plus substantial tip, Mae, seemingly the favoured customer, takes over.

The result is mixed. Mae first establishes that the young woman regularly works evenings at the bar. But she has no recollection of the name. Not that we're surprised. She must serve a lot of people whose names she doesn't know. And, of course, we have no description to offer.

Mae tries her luck with 'Philippe Jean, *de la Martinique*.'

The bartender smiles broadly. '*Oui, oui,* Philippe Jean.'

For a second I expect her to produce some fashion trinket. But no.

'*C'est chez moi.*'

It's at her house. Not yet cold enough to wear it, Mae tells me.

A friggin' neck gaiter. Like the girl in the museum in Grand Bank. Obviously the bartender doesn't realize it doubles as a scrunchie. Then again, her hair is too short. But my God, is there no end to the fashion designer's largesse.

The girl is blatantly excited to be telling Mae this. But no recollection of Philippe Jean talking to any one person. Apparently he talked to a lot of people, a lot of young men in particular. That does absolutely nothing to narrow the field.

Our time is up. The bartender needs to move on to another customer. Mae and I relocate to a table. The beer provides limited consolation.

Nick enters alone. Unsmiling, but looking better than expected. He takes a seat at the table.

'What can I get you?'

'I'm good, thanks.'

'You're sure?'

'I want to be of help,' he says. 'I want to help find the bastard.'

I'm unsure how to react. There's a vehemence that I can appreciate, but it can't be the controlling factor. He'll need to retain a level head in all this if he's going to get more involved.

He presses me. 'What can I do? Tell me and I'll do it.'

Mae can see I'm having trouble. 'It's going slowly,' she says to Nick. 'Your father is following a couple of leads. We have to see where they take us before we can do much more.'

He turns back to me. 'Leads, like what?'

I have no choicc. 'We think we know where Zach's swim trunks came from.'

'Tell me.'

'Nick, man, take it easy. Of course we'll tell you. But remember this is still early in the game. We can't be jumping to conclusions. There's a lot more we need to find out.'

'I know. Just tell me.'

I do. Against my better judgment at this point.

He says nothing. He's thinking, as if trying to fit the name in somewhere prior to the events on the beach. 'I think I know who you mean. I think I saw him.'

The surprise gives way to a need for something other than conjecture. 'Are you sure?'

'Black, dressed a bit loud for Saint-Pierre. Right here in this bar, last Saturday night. Three of us went out for a few beers. The guy we saw had to be him.'

'Fits the picture. But Saint-Pierre gets loads of tourists, a lot off cruise ships. People from everywhere, for sure some of them end up in Le Rustique. Was there any indication he could have been from Martinique? How close did you actually get to him?'

'Urinal to urinal.'

'I see.'

'As I was standing next to him, I did notice his baseball cap.'

'Really?' In my world the general rule in such situations is to completely ignore the other guy, pretend he doesn't exist.

'He was wearing his baseball cap backwards. It had flag decal. A flag I didn't recognize. Remember in grade eight I did this project on flags of the world? I thought I knew them all.'

'Really, your urinary focus is the flag on the cap of the dude next to you?' Humour is not without its place.

'Dad.'

'Was this it?' Mae is holding up her phone so we can both see its screen. Red triangle meeting two bands, one green, one black.

'Yeah, that's it exactly.'

'There's a reason you didn't recognize it. Martinique didn't adopt the flag until this year.'

'So it *was* him.'

'And by the way,' she adds, 'the cruise ship season ended here a week ago.' Mae and Google are an amazing combination.

Okay. There we have it. Confirmed—Philippe Jean was at Le Rustique Saturday evening. Yet to be confirmed—contact with one Johnny Smith.

'Who was he talking to? Anyone in your group?'

I'm wondering of course if Le Rustique is also where he made contact with Zach. Wondering, but not about to suggest it.

'Not unless it was at the bar. He didn't come around our table. We were sitting close to the door. I remember him passing by, on his way outside, him and some other guy. I remember because they were speaking English.'

'Any idea who?' A unilingual Johnny Smith, I'm thinking.

'No clue.'

'Anyone at your table recognize the other guy?' Mae asks. 'Zach maybe?'

'Zach wasn't there. He didn't come till later. He had work he wanted to do on his essay. By the time he showed up they were gone.'

Not surprisingly, by this point Nick has questions of his own. Which, when boiled down, amount to, 'Just why the heck are you guys asking me all this?'

'We found out that Philippe Jean met someone here, maybe that night, someone who might be able to shed some light on the business of the swim trunks, how Zach came to be wearing them.'

As Mae points out, 'We can't ask Philippe Jean himself because we know he's already left Saint-Pierre, and we presume, is back in Martinique.'

'We're thinking this other fellow might know and could still be around. We've been led to believe his name is Johnny Smith.'

A solid answer, without the accessory detail that might further upset him.

'You both think this guy Philippe Jean is gay, right?'

I hadn't expected that. It leaves me struggling to read Nick's mind. Is he now thinking that if Philippe Jean is gay, then there might have been a personal connection between him and Zach? I'm not about to go there. That could shatter him.

'Hadn't considered it really.' If it takes a lie, it takes a lie.

'I don't believe you.'

'It's true.'

'Listen Dad. Don't play games, okay. Be up front with me, okay. I'm not a kid anymore.'

And I can't be the protective father? I can only let the truth mess with him, when he's barely holding it together as it is?

I look at Nick, still taking shape as a man, experience having abruptly deepened the untroubled son I knew a few days ago. How much more truth can he take before it breaks him?

'Maybe he *is* gay. We have no way of knowing.'

'And you think he was attracted to Zach?'

'Possibly.'

'And Zach went along with it. Jesus.' His relative calm founders.

'Hold on, hold on, we don't know that. What we do know is that Philippe Jean talked to this guy Johnny Smith. Maybe he and Zach knew each other.'

'Zach and I were close, we were more than fuckin' best friends. He told me nothing about any of this shit about that guy.'

He's on the verge of losing it. Mae stretches out her hand and presses it against his. 'There's a lot we don't know that your father is trying to find out. It all takes time. We need you to hang in there. As hard as it is, we need you to do that.'

She gets up from her chair and hugs him. I'm staring at Nick with all the empathy in the world, but I'm not the one hugging him. He doesn't need the embarrassment of both of us doing it in public.

When Mae sits back down he's looking at me. There's something positive working its way through his torment. 'Man, you better do a good job.'

There's no stopping me. I get to him and clutch him in my arms.

And whisper in his ear. 'Fuckin' well right I will.'

SIX

IT'S OUR LAST few hours in Saint-Pierre. By mid-afternoon we're due aboard the ferry that will land us back in Newfoundland. The ferry is now on its reduced fall schedule, which means the next crossing is two days away, too long to wait. Mae has work commitments. As for the unpaid PI, extending my stay won't be the best use of my time, or fall within my budget. I'll go back home and forge ahead remotely. Maybe show up again if Nick uncovers something critical.

Which all points to the need to get myself in gear and tie up some loose ends. It's 7:20 a.m. and we're already at breakfast. Seated alone drinking coffee, as Pascal adds a tray of pastries to the buffet.

Satisfied that all its components are in attractive order, he stops by our table. '*L'avenir appartient à ceux qui se lèvent tôt.*'

No, Pascal, my French hasn't improved that much since I arrived. He looks at Mae, thinking he might have better luck. I'm afraid not.

'You say something about an early bird and a worm, which I don't understand.'

'Whatever you said I don't understand it either. Now we're even.'

He chuckles. I'm restless this morning, but managing to maintain a sense of humour that spans the language barrier.

'Speaking of a bird and a worm,' he says. 'I may have caught one.'

I'm not sure what sense that makes, but, 'Give it a go, *monsieur*.' I take another shot of caffeine.

'I had a call last evening asking if Philippe Jean was still a guest at the *auberge*. When I said no, the woman hung up immediately.'

I set the coffee mug down firmly. 'Any idea who it could have been?'

'None. When I answered I assumed it was someone wanting to make a reservation.'

'No caller ID?'

'Just a number. Which I'm afraid I can't recall exactly, except I did notice the area code.'

'Which was?'

'709. We get a lot of reservations from Newfoundland and Labrador.'

'No idea of the next three digits?' Which, if it were a landline, would at least point us to a specific part of the province.

'I wasn't paying that much attention. I was anxious to finish up for the night.'

Understandable . . . But do I have to ask the obvious? In fact, I do.

'Would you mind looking up the recent calls to your phone?'

He hesitates. 'Normally I treat phone records as confidential.'

'You did tell us someone called.'

'So I did.'

He's of two minds still. My bet is he's wondering what repercussions there might be for his *auberge* if a vile, potentially vengeful caller were to find out he had released her number to a *détective privé*.

It appears my only choice is to play the ace. 'We are, after all, dealing with (and this is *highly* confidential by the way) . . . we are dealing with a murder investigation.'

Pascal is sufficiently dumbstruck that he extracts his phone from his pocket.

'The pastries are delicious by the way,' says Mae. Good move. It takes the edge of the tension. I have my notepad out and pen in hand.

When all is said and done, Pascal delivers. Hesitantly, but suitably clear. Seven digits dictated.

Another couple of guests enter the room. We have never met, but greetings are exchanged all around, reserved but pleasantly polite, very French.

As Pascal wanders over to have a few more words with them, Mae takes out her phone. I position the open notebook in front of her. She is already into Canada 411 reverse phone lookup.

'Unlisted.' Grimace. 'Landline.' Eyebrows raised.

'857 exchange?'

'Lamaline, Newfoundland.'

Eyes open wide. 'No kidding.'

She puts down her phone. 'And we both know who lived in Lamaline.'

'As still do his mother and father, presumably.'

Which leaves us both with the same questions. Could Zach's parents have somehow found out about Philippe Jean? Which would be very odd if they did. Why, for any reason, would Zach have told them?

Questions that can only be answered by showing up in Lamaline and tracking down the couple, in the hope they would agree to talk with us about their son. Our return to St. John's will include a purposeful detour.

That's for tomorrow. As for the immediate course of events—more cups of coffee, granola, yoghurt, pastries one and two. All sustenance needed to face the potentially dodgy Amélie. Prior to, later in the morning, the potentially wide-eyed Tremblay and Charpentier.

Our immediate destination: Île aux Marins. A return to the isle of the crime.

Our actual destination: Chez Anne-Laure. A return to the residence of the woman we both believe knows much more than she's offered up as yet.

How far we'll get with this is anyone's guess, given the fact that at the headquarters of the *gendarmerie* we pulled the plug on Amélie and her GoPro (against my better judgment, I will add).

Mae is innocently hopeful. Experience has taught me that having alienated the potential informant, you're in for a rough ride should you show up on her doorstep acting as if nothing has happened.

Chez Anne-Laure is as turquoise as ever, larger than life. Not exactly a place to be living if your aim is to blend in with the landscape, which could be taken as a point in Amélie's favour. She's not out to hide her presence, if in fact she's still inside.

There is only one way to find out. A solid yet non-threatening knock.

We wait. No response.

Slight increase in the decibel level of the knock. We wait.

The door opens. '*Bonjour.*' It is not Amélie.

It's Théo. He fills most of the doorway while a gentle smile fills much of his face.

'*Bonjour*,' is our inept chorus.

But I don't think he recognizes us. We weren't that close to each other on the beach, and his focus was on Amélie and the victim. Plus, I had the benefit of the GoPro's zoom function.

'*Nous recherchons Amélie Dubois,*' Mae tells him expeditiously, returning his smile.

There's no hesitation. '*Un moment.*' He disappears inside, calling Amélie's name.

I look at Mae. I assume we have the same thought—Théo is not in as much shit as we had expected. Either the cops went easy on him, or for some reason the GoPro footage didn't make it into their hands. Add that to our list of unanswered questions.

Amélie is slow to make it to the door. She arrives with wet hair and an apologetic look. It quickly stiffens to one of indignation.

'Amélie, how are you?' Not overly cheery, but pleasant, hopeful.

'I'm fine.'

There is nothing about her look to confirm it.

I cut past the preliminaries. 'We have some questions.'

'Questions?'

'*Oui, des questions.*'

'I don't need your translation.'

A further upsurge in tension.

'Why the fuck should I be answering your questions?'

The upsurge just hit the roof.

'I'm a private investigator. I have questions concerning the murder of Zach Russell. I would take your lack of co-operation as indication that you are holding back something that is central to the investigation.'

'Théo!'

Théo arrives at warp speed, meaning he was so close he had to be listening in on the conversation. He looms behind Amélie.

I ram past her intimidation tactics. 'Your GoPro footage must have been quite helpful to Colonel Tremblay.'

'What fucking footage?' she fires back, coupled with searing eye contact from Théo.

'The footage you showed me.'

'I didn't show you any fucking footage except him and his fucking trunks.'

This is going nowhere fast.

Mae interjects. 'In which case you deleted any footage of *les Sauveteurs en Mer*.'

'In which case you mind your own fucking business.'

Nobody speaks. It could be something of a cooling-off period. It's not.

It's a break to suck in a breath and decide where to take it from here.

Amélie has played innocent to Tremblay and Charpentier. She knew we likely told them about *les Sauveteurs en Mer*, so what was her story? That Théo and his pals were nearby on exercises and happened upon the scene? That she thought the fellow in the water might still be alive so she put out a call to them? But once they examined the body and confirmed Zach was dead, she told Théo and company to back off?

She could have fabricated any number of scenarios to keep the boyfriend in the clear. And, what the hell, she could even have played us up as potential liars. I can just hear her telling Tremblay and Charpentier she had no idea what we were up to before she showed up on the beach.

I jack up the heat. 'What do you know about a guy named Philippe Jean? Did he happen to spend a night in Chez Anne-Laure? You better come clean or this time you'll definitely be in deep shit.'

Suddenly she's a deer in the headlights. She glances back at the looming presence behind her. Théo's language skills are just enough to envenom him at the thought of another guy in Amélie's life.

She's wrestling with what to say.

'And a guy named Johnny Smith?' I add. 'Did he also spend a night in Chez Anne-Laure?' Théo's venom thickens.

Do I push the envelope even further? Do I outright lie to get what I'm after?

'I'm wondering if Jean and Johnny were into threesomes.'

It is not a lie exactly. Just wondering, that's all.

Mae stiffens. Théo's fangs are out.

Amélie explodes. 'Bullfuckingshit!'

Her English is more accomplished than I anticipated.

'But Philippe Jean, from Martinique—you know who I'm talking about. Right?'

'No!'

She's lying. I know it. 'What if the cops were to question Philippe Jean and he said he did know you? What then?'

'Like hell. You're saying the cops would go to Martinique on your guesswork? Not fucking likely.'

Why would she assume he's back in Martinique? Unless Philippe Jean himself told her he was going. Keep her talking and she'll blow the whistle on herself even louder.

Unfortunately not. With a resounding 'Fuck right off!' she slams the door in our faces.

Whoa. That was a hullabaloo and a half.

Mae and I have no fallback. We wander away in the direction of the dock to wait for the ferry's next return trip.

Plenty of time to ruminate on what we just witnessed.

'Two things,' Mae says. 'She obviously speaks better English than she first let on. And second, I'm not sure she had anything to do with Johnny Smith. Philippe Jean maybe, although bringing sex into it was a stretch.'

'Investigative technique, Mae.'

'It did trigger an emphatic end to the conversation. She'll never have anything more to do with you.'

'It was worth it. She definitely linked herself to Philippe Jean.'

'Maybe.'

'No maybe about it.'

'I'm not sure you can assume that just because she made reference to Philippe Jean being back in Martinique she had much to do with him.'

She's wrong. I'd bet my life on it.

I don't respond. I know to stop before Mae digs in her heels. I swallow my argument.

We're not on the same page. That's the last thing we need. I sure don't want it messing up the meeting I set up with the cops to get the go-ahead to leave Saint-Pierre.

'I think you should just go on your own,' she says now that the ferry has docked and we've started walking in the direction of the police station.

A relatively muted, introspective ferry crossing has led to this. I think she's right.

'It should be your show. I don't need to tag along.'

No need to go that far. What's with the "tag along"?

'We're in this together.'

'To some extent.'

I expect more. There's nothing, putting the onus back on me. Which I don't think is entirely fair.

I leave it. Let it stand as is. Meet the cops on my own while she hangs back and does whatever she wants to do. Have a coffee, go shopping, whatever. She doesn't tell me.

My head is not entirely where it needs to be as I approach the entrance to the police station. I check my phone. Definitely no time to regroup and review my approach to the two-on-one that lies squarely in front of me.

I'm directed to the colonel's office. Tremblay is at his desk, a laptop open before him. Charpentier leans over his shoulder, his eyes also on the screen.

They both straighten up. We shake hands. Tremblay points to a chair in front of the desk. I sit down, and Charpentier does the same to the left of the colonel.

I get ahead of their questions. 'Thank you, gentlemen. My partner is otherwise occupied. As you know our intention is to take the ferry back to Newfoundland later today. You're good with that I assume?' Putting it in such a way that all it requires is a simple "yes."

'I guess so.'

The next best thing. 'In which case I thought it would be useful to compare notes before leaving Saint-Pierre.'

'Compare notes?'

Either he doesn't understand the phrase or he's questioning whether there's good reason to exchange information. Let's be positive and assume it's the former.

As I'm about to clarify my choice of words, the colonel adds, 'I assume you have something more to tell us in regard to the investigation. Please, go right ahead, Mr. *Synard*.' Mispronouncing my name.

I'm left wondering if he takes this meeting to be a one-way street. But no, let's remain positive.

'Since our last encounter, gentlemen, considerably more information has been uncovered about Philippe Jean.' I proceed to relate it in detail, pausing to allow the colonel to translate when Charpentier looks particularly confounded.

I could be kind and call their combined reactions politely neutral. Or be less kind and call them lukewarm, verging on dismissive.

I smell apathy. And if there's one thing you don't expect of a cop it's effing apathy.

'That's all very interesting, Mr. *Synard*. But again, it shouldn't come as a surprise that our focus is elsewhere.'

One would think that with so many *gendarmes* on the

payroll there would be opportunity for several goddamn foci.

Calm down, Synard. You're in a foreign country. You play by their rules. You keep a lid on it.

'I see. Just to clarify however, my name is pronounced Synard. As in "innard." Synard . . . innard.' (As in "guts," which I don't add because there's no way he'd have a sweet friggin' clue why I said it.)

'I see. I'll do my best.' With a thin edge of irritation.

Suitably steeled, I press on with the matter of one Johnny Smith. My words are left hanging in the air. If I didn't know better I would say the officers are dumbstruck.

'You believe this Johnny Smith might have a direct connection to the death of Zach Russell?'

'There is a strong possibility.'

'On what evidence?'

'Like Zach, he's connected to Philippe Jean. Therefore, there's a strong possibility he and Zach encountered each other.'

'On the beach in Île aux Marins?'

'Exactly.'

'Are you suggesting this Johnny Smith carried a knife, with the intention of stabbing Zach Russell?'

'That is a possibility, yes.'

'What has led you to that conclusion?'

'The fact that any personal items belonging to Zach are missing.'

'I don't see the connection.'

These rapid-fire responses have upped the tension. Tremblay has dispensed with any pauses to translate for Charpentier. His eyes rest solely on me.

'I'm still working on the connection.'

'Pure speculation therefore.'

'Pure is too strong a word.'

As a comeback, a bit below par, I admit.

Tremblay is not impressed. 'Mr. *Synard* . . . excuse me . . . Mr. Synard, let's be clear. You have taken this on for no reason, this amateur investigation. My advice to you is to leave it in the hands of the police. If you want to keep in touch, that's fine, I will give you my email address. If there is something pertaining to our investigation that we are willing to disclose then I will. I know your son has been traumatized and wants to know how and why his friend died, but the process takes time. Lieutenant Charpentier and his team are working nonstop. Leave it in their hands. Return home and try to put it out of your mind.'

At the mention of his name, Charpentier springs to life. '*Oui*, out of your mind.'

A firestorm rears in my gut.

'Colonel Tremblay, let *me* be clear.' As restrained as I can make it. 'I happen to be a licensed private investigator.' I turn quickly to Charpentier. 'A *détective privé, monsieur*.' Then back to Tremblay, 'I assume there is no law in France that outlaws individuals such as myself. In which case I have every right . . .'

'Excuse me, *Monsieur Synard*.'

He is clearly surprised. I'd say flummoxed. We'll just see how he deals with this bolt out of the blue.

'Licensed by whom? By CNAPS?'

Let's not get cryptic.

'CNAPS—*Conseil national des activités privées de sécurité*.'

'Really.'

'It regulates private security in our country. Unless you are licensed by CNAPS you are . . . I believe the English term is "out of luck."'

Okay . . . so I'm compromised. And he knows it. Maybe thinking I'm up shit creek, if he had better grasp of the language.

'Let me be firm. You are required by law to bring your investigation to an end.'

Without a paddle.

What do I say to that? Nothing decent comes to mind.

I straighten up and stand up. I refuse to look or sound intimidated. 'Thank you, gentlemen, for your valuable time. In due course I will be back in touch. At which point I will be in Canada, in my own jurisdiction. If, at that time, I uncover something that I deem to be valuable to you, I will of course pass it along. In the meantime, I wish you well in your investigation. *Bonne chance.*' I pause to quickly shake hands. 'And, as I like to say—*hasta la vista*.'

And on that note, the colonel hands me his business card. I take it, turn, and make my own way out of the building.

The air is clear. The sun is shining. It feels good to have that behind me and move on to more practical use of my time.

I text Mae and once she's replied I make my way to *Square Joffre*. She's seated on the bench where we sat yesterday. Beside her is one of those classy paper shopping bags with ribbon handles. 'I bought a little something for myself.'

She's also brought two cappuccinos. Very good. I can use the caffeine boost.

And a small box of pastries she calls *cannelés*. I sit next to her. She offers the open box and I take one. Small, with a caramelized crust and the taste of rum.

She doesn't question how it went with the police, leaving it up to me to reassure her. 'All good to go.'

'No conflict?'

I had decided on dodging the more contentious bit. But now that I'm actually sitting next to Mae, I'm no longer sure it's worth the risk. 'If I put off telling you, I'll likely get more than just desserts.'

Prodigious pun aside, I take the bull by the horns and man up.

'Well,' I tell her, 'somewhat less than good.'

Again she doesn't question. Which doesn't mean she won't scrutinize whatever I come up with.

I divulge my lack of legal standing. 'There it is.'

She holds off. Only for a moment. 'I don't see you have much choice.'

A bit more sympathy would have been preferable.

'What do you do now?'

"You," I notice, not "we."

'We carry on. Once we land back in Newfoundland all restrictions are off.'

'I thought you intended to return here to follow up on anything Nick might come up with.'

'We'll see. That depends.' I'm not sure on what.

I finish the coffee in one sustained guzzle and stand up. Mae has not quite finished hers, but she hands me her cup, then puts the box with the remaining *cannelés* in her tote while I find a place to dispose of the cups. We're due to meet Nick for one final get-together before catching the ferry.

He's waiting outside the Francoforum. He has two hours before classes resume in the afternoon, enough time for an extended lunch. Our suggestion is the restaurant attached to Hotel Robert, where legend has it that Al Capone stayed while on a visit during Prohibition.

'According to Zach there's no solid evidence that Al Capone ever visited Saint-Pierre.'

He said it without much emotional residue. Good for him.

Nick has other ideas where we should have lunch. 'Remember you intended to meet Emmeline. She said you're still welcome to come by. Today would be good. She's making soup. There'll be plenty.'

I had planned on something more private, this being the last time I'll see him for a while. On the other hand, it would be good to establish a relationship with Emmeline, considering the support she can give Nick to make it through the term.

Emmeline is older, a widow, and speaks no English. She's also endearing, a fine cook, and speaks French with a speed that leaves me smiling doltishly. Mae fares only a little better.

Nick, I'm proud to say, is able to carry on a spontaneous conversation, as are the other two students who are boarding with Emmeline and have joined us at the table. If my ear is telling me anything it's that Nick's French is the least accented. An incentive, I hope, to up his language skills even more by sticking with the program.

At the moment he is also acting as translator for his deficient father. When we're far enough into the meal that everyone seems comfortable with each other, I have a question. Not one that I expect to go anywhere, but one worth asking on the off chance it strikes a chord with someone.

'Does the name Johnny Smith mean anything to you? A young man from Newfoundland who has been in Saint-Pierre recently, maybe not a tourist.'

Both students give it a quick no. Nick translates for Emmeline, and once she gets past the abruptness of the question, quietly shakes her head, sorry she can't be helpful.

Seemingly on second thought she directs a question of her own to Nick, one intended for me. Does the man have a relative living in Saint-Pierre, someone whose name she might recognize?

I'm not sure where she's going with that.

Emmeline explains that there are a number of Newfoundland women who married men from Saint-Pierre and now live here permanently. Perhaps Johnny Smith is related to one of them.

I admit that hadn't crossed my mind. 'Could be.'

Emmeline says she'll ask around. She has a married friend in Saint-Pierre who came from Newfoundland. Her name wasn't

Smith, but she would be friends with several other women from her home province. Maybe one of them was a Smith.

There you go. You take a chance and this is what happens.

It might lead nowhere. But then again it might not.

'*Merci, madame. Très bonne idée.*'

It's Nick's good luck to have Emmeline as his *mère française*. And my good luck to have her as my temporary co-investigator *française*.

Take that, CNAPS, and put it where the *soleil* don't shine.

I catch Mae's eye. She shares my enthusiasm, tentatively at least.

As does Nick, as the three of us walk back to the Francoforum. 'This will be in your hands. Obviously I won't be able to communicate with Emmeline directly.'

It offers him a role in the investigation, likewise under the radar. I'm hoping it will reinforce his decision to stay in Saint-Pierre, make him feel he's doing something useful in finding the answer to what happened to his friend.

'One way or another we have to find the bastard who did it.'

Strong language from a son who not so long ago was just a kid. It hurts like hell that he should have to face all this instead of being left to revel in life as a university student. I remember those years—away from home, unfettered from adolescence, not yet restrained by adulthood.

I want him past all that's happened, but I realize for now his peace of mind is a long way off. And I realize too that, far more than I wish it were, his life is in his own hands.

We've reached the point where we have to part ways. Pascal has brought our luggage from the *auberge* to the terminal, and with our copious thanks, left again.

I look at Nick and believe I can confirm he's more accepting of his decision to finish out the program. Yet I won't be worrying about him any less.

'I'm as close as your phone. Day or night.' I hug him long and hard.

'I'll be okay,' he says quietly, before turning to Mae.

I think I believe him. Our texts and calls should tell me if he's otherwise. I have contact information for Sasha at the Francoforum if I need another point of view.

I'm unusually quiet as we're crossing to Fortune. Mae notices, but doesn't question it. It takes the relative closeness of the Newfoundland coastline to bring me back to something closer to the fellow she knows.

The accommodation at Hotel Fortune is entirely fine, as is the meal at the Stage Head Café. But my mind is somewhere else.

Then, as we're walking back to the hotel, I get a text from Nick. Emmeline's inquiries have gone nowhere. 'So far,' he's said. I like his optimism but I have doubts it's warranted.

There's little more to do but sit in the hotel room and ruminate.

Mae looks at me, clearly wanting to talk, but waiting for me to start the exchange.

'I have no way to take this business about Philippe Jean any further. The thing with Johnny Smith probably amounts to bugger all. The French cops want nothing to do with me.'

'You're worried about Nick. It's thrown you off. You're over-anxious about getting somewhere with the investigation. It takes time.'

Let's be honest, she's not appreciating how frustrating it is to be in a friggin' rut when what you need is a path to at least move ahead.

We stop at that and go to bed. The distance between us now, consciously or not, a physical one.

A night's rest can work wonders. Not in this case.

'You did a lot of tossing and turning.'

Not that I need reminding. I keep the grumbling to myself. It helps that the room is still dark except for a night light near the coffee maker. Mae has already put it to use. I'm known to be more civil once I have caffeine in me.

'I'm sorry.' I pour a coffee and take to the empty armchair. 'I kept you awake.'

'I'm fine.'

'It's only a half-hour to Lamaline. We don't want to arrive too early. Maybe we'll look for some place to have breakfast.'

'I had a couple of the leftover *cannelés*. The last two are in the box for you. I think I might just go back to bed for a while.'

Fair enough. As I reach for the box she discards her robe and lays it across the armchair she's been sitting in. She's wearing what can only be the "little something" she bought in Saint-Pierre. A little nothing-left-to-the-imagination negligee.

She peels it off and lays it over the robe, before stepping along the side of the bed and slipping naked between the covers.

I finish chewing and swallow hard. When you least expect it. I linger on the second *cannelé* and finish with more caffeine.

She's feeling sorry for me. She's hitting on my lack of self-control. She's pursuing diversionary tactics.

But what the fuck.

Lamaline is an unhurried, untroubled drive. I hate to think my mental makeup was so simply reconfigured, at the whim of libido. I seriously doubt it.

Regardless, I'm not about to give myself a hard time. Relax. Enjoy the consequences as long as they last. Hum . . . even sing a little.

'Lamaline, Lamaline / Prettiest town I've ever seen / Women there don't treat you mean / in Lamaline, my Lamaline.'

Lamaline is one of those Newfoundland outports that entices me to substitute its name in the lyrics of a song. That one goes way back. A country classic.

Mae is greatly amused. I have more.

'You know the preacher liked the cold / He knows I'm gonna stay / Catalina dreamin' / On such a winter's day.'

Nick would love this. We'd be driving somewhere, just Nick and me, and we'd launch into it, trying to outdo each other.

'Ah-hoo, werewolves of Lomond / Ah-hoo / Ah-hoo werewolves of Lomond / Ah-hoo!'

Mae's more than amused.

'First we take Makinsons, then we take Berlin.'

I wish Nick were around to hear this.

Google Maps doesn't do Lamaline justice, but it's enough to lead us to the TNT Snack Shack. Where the cook doing the prep for her day of chicken, fries, and gravy takes time to give us directions.

She's absolutely right, we couldn't have missed it. Up Lodge Road and not far from St. Mary the Virgin Anglican Church. As she said, if we had gone as far as the Seaview Spa we would have had to turn back. We don't go that far, intrigued though we are that someone would build a spa in Lamaline, population: 218.

The house is set well back from the road, a hefty red pickup parked next to it. I turn into the driveway and come to a stop partway along it, to give Zach's parents the opportunity to see us walk up to the house. The moment we exit the car a dog starts barking, its head above what appears to be the back of a couch. It brings the figure of a woman to the window. She withdraws quickly.

She's at the front door as we approach it. I presume it's Mrs. Russell. She opens the door enough to ask, rather numbly, 'May I help you?'

I'm assuming the police referred to us when they broke the news of her son's death. We introduce ourselves, but to judge by her unchanged expression, our names were lost in the trauma of the moment.

'I'm Nick Synard's father. Nick was a friend of your son in Saint-Pierre. They did French together.'

By this time her husband has arrived, with the muted but still distrustful dog in his arms. The man is about my height, but considerably heavier. His sweatshirt covers a thick midsection.

'You're the couple who found Zach. I recognize you from the picture Zach sent after the meal.'

Mrs. Russell immediately wells up.

'That was us. Together with Nick.'

'We're so sorry for what happened to your son,' Mae tells them.

'What did happen?' responds the father. 'That's what we need to know.'

Stress is controlling the encounter. We will have to find a way past it if Zach's parents are going to come around to answering our questions.

'We are more than willing to share what we know. Perhaps we can be of help to you. May we come in?'

It's rather forward of me, but they're clearly desperate for answers. Although, to be honest, I'm not sure we have any more than the police will have offered.

Nevertheless, the door is opened wider. We are led to the living room and to the couch that backs against the window. Only at that point do they introduce themselves—Brian and Lisa. They look to be a little younger than us.

Their lives suddenly shattered, they are dealing with it as best they can. Together with their dog, Jack. I know the breed.

A good-looking mutt, seemingly no less active than normal. A distraction for them, I hope.

Jack, the Jack Russell terrier—only now does it strike me. 'Jack Russell,' I say to the dog, 'how convenient is that?' It breaks the ice somewhat, and at the mention of his name, we seem to have endeared ourselves to Jack. He wanders over for a lick of our outstretched hands.

For the most part Lisa and Brian remain sombre, with the expectation that we redirect our attention to the serious matter that allowed us into their home.

As gently as we can, we recount our discovery of the body. It is laden with emotion. In time the parents compose themselves enough to turn their attention to what else we have to say.

'Our son, Nick, and Zach were very good friends. Nick has been terribly upset, as you can imagine.'

'Zach talked about him like they were more than friends,' comments Brian.

I glance at Mae. It is hard to judge, but I'm thinking she is no less surprised than I am.

'Zach was gay,' Brian adds.

My preconceived notions of outport attitudes fly out the window. What appears to be open acceptance of their son's orientation is refreshing, but I have to admit, unexpected.

'Zach came out to us more than a year ago,' Brian says.

'Almost two years now,' inserts his wife.

'We were upset at first, but it didn't last long. He is our son, and we weren't about to turn our backs on him.'

'He meant the world to us,' Lisa says, and wells up again. 'He was a wonderful young man.' The tears flow freely.

Brian puts an arm around her shoulders before turning back and looking intently at me. 'You think being gay had anything to do with his death?'

He's asking father-to-father. We both have heard stories of the violence, the hate crimes. One likes to think society has moved beyond it or that at least it wouldn't have found its way into rural Newfoundland, or in this case Saint-Pierre.

'Not as far as I know.' Not that it has been something I've focused on.

'What does Nick think?'

I'm reluctant to admit we haven't talked about it. My unease is showing.

'Nick hasn't said much,' Mae inserts. 'At this point at least. He's still so upset. And we're not sure if the French police are aware . . .'

'I told them.'

Also unexpected. 'And what was their response?'

'Hard to tell.'

'Communicating with the French police is not easy,' I note, 'as you've probably discovered.'

'They said they'll be back in touch when they get the results of the autopsy.'

'Which is taking time, since it is being performed in Paris, which I'm sure must have come as a bit of a shock to you both.'

'We've had to accept it. We have no choice.'

His solemn bluntness I'm still dealing with.

'We were contacted by the Canadian Embassy in Paris. They told us that when the time comes to transport the body back to Canada everything will be done with great respect.'

Even as his wife struggles to contain her emotions, Brian has somehow found a way to control his. It has only been a few days since they found out. I'm not sure I would be so stoic.

He seems to sense what is going through my mind. 'I lost my father,' he says, 'when I was twelve. He died of silicosis and lung cancer, from working in the mine in St. Lawrence. It was a slow death, and very painful.'

The long-term exposure of men to silica dust in the fluorspar mines of St. Lawrence is well documented. Brian was one of the children whose lives were forever changed by its consequences. Perhaps that loss helped Brian face what has happened to his son, or perhaps it has only helped him suppress his grief.

We look at each other, fathers who have known the immeasurable joy sons have instilled in their lives.

'What *can* you tell us?' he asks.

Implying that we haven't told them much so far that they don't already know. That they have invited us into their home with very little to show for it.

It is time I bring Philippe Jean into the conversation. It only causes confusion. They have no idea where Martinique is or why such a stranger would suddenly be a focus for what happened to their son.

'All because of a pair of swimming trunks? Is the fellow gay? Was he trying to put the makes on Zach?'

I don't have anything definite to offer in response to either one of them. 'Possibly.'

That does nothing for Brian. 'Zach wouldn't have broken trust with your son. I know Zach. He'd never have gotten involved with that guy. He would have told him to fuck right off.'

So much for the thread of that conversation.

'Lisa, I have a question.' Mae intercedes, saving me the trouble of figuring out where to take things from here. I ignore her tone of voice. I know, I know—she's not keen that the women have largely been left out of the discussion so far. It wasn't intentional.

'Does the name Johnny Smith mean anything to you?'

Lisa is quick to respond. 'My first cousin. Once removed.'

A freakin' jolt and a half.

Mae recovers faster than I do. 'Could he have been in Saint-Pierre sometime over the last couple of days?'

'I wouldn't be surprised.'

She stops, catching the look her husband has cast her way. She's suddenly tight-lipped.

Brian is not pleased. 'Whataya asking for?' He's taken on a new posture. One that's looking a little hostile.

'The name came up,' I tell him. 'He's somehow connected to Philippe Jean.'

'There's a thousand Johnny Smiths.'

It goes without saying the one who has a connection to Zach's mother and therefore Zach is of particular interest.

A bit of a standoff.

'You're friggin' telling me that Johnny had something to do with whatever happened to Zach.'

'A connection, Brian. At this point nothing more than a possible connection. Perhaps entirely innocent, but a connection nonetheless. One that needs to be clarified.'

'You sound like a cop.'

'I assure you I am not a cop.'

'What then? Why did you show up here asking all these questions?'

Lisa's upset is again audible. Mae's instinct is to comfort her.

Not at this point. 'Besides being Nick's father, I happen to be a private investigator.'

That brings it all to a standstill. A more intense sob from Lisa amplifies the tension.

'We're very sorry if we upset you more than you already are,' Mae says quietly. 'That's the last thing you need. What Sebastian wants you to know is that he's doing all he can to help find an explanation for what happened to your son. Yes, as it turns out, he works as a private investigator. But he is first and foremost a parent. Just as both of you are.' She pauses, briefly. 'We met Zach. As you know we all had supper together the day we arrived in Saint-Pierre. A fine young man indeed. Our only motive in coming here today is to help bring an understanding of what happened to Zach the next morning. If that is the case, then I hope we will have done some good. That's all.'

I might have said the same thing, though not likely with the same control. There's a lot to be said for the measured approach, especially when you're dealing with an overwrought mother.

As Mae now again demonstrates. She walks across the room to Lisa, bends over, and gives her a sustained hug. Such is the female advantage.

It would not do any good for me to walk over and even so much as lay a hand on Brian's shoulder. I'd likely have it unceremoniously flung back at me.

Mae withdraws from Lisa and—albeit very briefly—hugs Brian.

All very well and good.

But where exactly does Mae expect us to go from here?

After seating herself back on the couch, she takes out her phone, and, having found what's she's looking for, looks across to Lisa and asks, 'Would you happen to recognize this phone number?'

The phone number disclosed to us by Pascal at Auberge Daguerre.

Lisa is silent. She turns to look at her husband.

He hesitates. The hostility seems to have increased. 'This is off the record. Nothing gets back to the cops in Saint-Pierre.'

In view of the weight of what could follow, I tolerate his look. I glance at Mae. I sense she can as well. In which case there is only one answer. 'Of course.'

He looks back at Lisa, and again at us. 'Johnny's mother. It's her number.'

Indeed. Heavy-duty.

He fires the inevitable 'Where did you get it?'

'A perfectly good question.'

Which does nothing to cool him down.

I press on. 'According to the owner of the guesthouse where Philippe Jean had stayed while he was on Saint-Pierre, a woman called from that number looking for him.'

'What did she have to do with him, whoever the fuck he is?'

Precisely.

'That we don't know,' I tell him, still unruffled. 'That's what we hope to find out.'

He looks at his wife. 'Call Rolinda. Call her right now and find out how she knows about whatever-the-fuck's-his-name.'

No matter how you put it, definitely not a good idea. Lisa springing this on Johnny's mother is bound to backfire on the investigation. Leaving me pissed that a crucial lead had slipped through my fingers.

'I wouldn't do that if I were you.'

Brian is in no mood to be contradicted. He glowers at me.

'I think it's better coming from us. We're the ones digging into the connection to Philippe Jean. You'd have a lot of explaining to do. We don't want Rolinda pissed off at you. We'll handle it.'

He's not convinced.

'Of course we'll report back to you both.'

'I think he's right,' says Lisa. 'Rolinda is hard enough to get along with as it is.'

He broods. But I'm thinking Lisa might have won him over. At least he doesn't say no.

Leaving us with the presumption that there's far more to Rolinda than meets the eye.

'I doubt if she'll tell you anything,' says Brian. He looks at Lisa. 'It's your side of the family.'

Which seems to be permission for his wife to add some background to Rolinda. And, I'm hoping, her son. My gut tells me the plot is about to thicken.

'Rolinda has her issues,' Lisa tells us. But hesitates to go further. She glances at Brian. He's stone-faced.

'Such as?' says Mae, quietly, smoothly. Woman to woman.

'With Johnny.'

We wait. She hesitates again. Mae decides against a second prompt.

Lisa takes a deep breath. At which point I dive in. 'Johnny is a bit of a laddio?'

Lisa eyes me, coldly. Lips tighter than ever.

Really? In Newfoundland "laddio" is not much of a step up from mischievous. Mild compared to what else I have in mind.

Brian looks about ready to erupt. He's doing his damndest to be civil. 'Tell him, Lise, for frig's sake, tell him.'

"Lise" could pass for a term of endearment. Unfortunately, the pitch of her husband's voice undercuts it. Lise closes her eyes tightly, pressing a tear onto her cheek.

'Johnny got busted twice for smuggling,' Brian blurts out. 'A year in the slammer and his truck seized, the stupid fucker.'

I'm off balance. More from the choice description of the guy than by what he was up to. Obviously there's no love lost between Brian and the misguided Johnny.

Off balance, but maybe not surprised. Lamaline is about as close as you can get to the French islands from Newfoundland, a quick dart in a speedboat with a couple of hefty outboards. No doubt the town's got a long history of smuggling cheap rum from Saint-Pierre. I would have thought Johnny's behaviour was inherited.

'Crack,' says Brian, 'the stupid fucker.'

Let's make that off balance *and* surprised.

Cocaine. Really? I don't ask, not wanting to sound like I'm just off the ark. I take it Johnny was caught smuggling crack *to* Saint-Pierre, not *from* Saint-Pierre.

'Shipped in from Ontario?' asks Mae, seemingly more clued in than I am.

Brian shrugs. 'Middleman for some wheeler-dealer in St. John's.'

'I'm not surprised,' says Mae. 'You go anywhere these days and you find dealers.'

A pretty broad statement there Mae.

'You can say that again,' says Brian.

At the risk of confirming I'm still in sight of the ark, I refrain from arguing the point. Of course drug-related crime is pervasive. We all know that. I'm just taken aback that smuggling alcohol from Saint-Pierre seems to have taken a back seat. It's had such a long and colourful history that I hate to see it happen. Dealing crack seems so much more sinister.

But there it is, you move with the times. The times now being where we confront Rolinda and Johnny Smith and find out just what the hell they've been up to with regard to Philippe Jean.

Time to set our encounter with Lisa and Brian to one side, and with their directions, make our way to the home of the Smiths for an unexpected visit, and more than likely, a combative reception.

Brian and I exchange contact information. He's the one to see us off, with Lisa in the background, still teary-eyed.

'Good luck,' he says, a perceptible edge of sarcasm emerging from beneath his still solemn exterior.

'We're doing this for Zach more than anyone,' I assure him.

He doesn't respond. At first, at least.

He's turned and is having a private moment with Lisa. He rejoins us, his expression unchanged.

'We'll pay you. If you find out who murdered Zach, we'll pay you.'

Nothing I was expecting. And nothing I quite know how to deal with.

Payment on condition of explicit results is not the way private investigation works.

'We'll talk.' The best I will do for now.

'We mean it,' he says. 'Whatever it takes. I had a decent year on the crab.'

So, Brian fishes snow crab. I hear commercial crab fishermen make good money. Considerably more than a tour guide/PI.

Whatever I'm doing for Zach, I'm also doing for Nick. Any payment from Brian and Lisa would be a dividend. If I want to look at it that way.

Not to be impractical. Everything else aside, I would put the money to good use.

'Take care.' My final words to the couple before the door is closed and we head for the Toyota, a vehicle well past its best-before date. Also red, it looks rather underfunded in contrast to the pickup it's parked behind.

SEVEN

WE'RE TAKING A breather. There's been a lot to assimilate before taking that thorny step in the path ahead.

Oddly, Mae and I don't say much. We drive reservedly through town, to the road leading to Allan's Island and its lighthouse. The island was once a separate community but is now joined by a causeway and considered part of Lamaline. On the way, drawing on Brian's directions, we pass what must be the Smith family home. Looking irreproachable, from the outside.

Lighthouses have taken on a peculiar aura after a recent tour I led for a group of four enigmatic lighthouse enthusiasts. The structures are beacons of hope, yet you never quite know what to expect when you get up close and personal. Mae and I divert our attention from the lighthouse to the seascape surrounding it. Surf pounding ashore can take your mind off what awaits inland.

For a time at least. Mae points out that during the Second World War, Allan's Island was home to a US Army early warning radar station, in case Nazis should heave into view. She alerts me, unintentionally I assume, to the fact that to be forewarned is to be forearmed.

'And did you know that the placename Lamaline is thought to be "a corruption of *la maligne*, a French term meaning malignant, evil, or wicked?"'

'Put away your phone, Mae, my love. Give it a rest.'

Let's keep our thoughts upbeat. '*Lamaline, Lamaline*,' I half-sing. '*Prettiest town I've ever seen . . .*'

Mae joins me, '*Women there don't treat you mean . . .*'

On the contrary.

'And just what the fuck do you want?'

It abruptly shatters the stereotype of the outport housewife and mother. That warm-hearted, lovable individual who greets strangers with a smile and the offer of cups of tea and freshly made molasses buns.

The whiff welling past the marginally open door is not of molasses buns. It's marijuana. That should have been my first clue. I shouldn't have been so gobsmacked by her response, having discreetly introduced myself and quietly noted my connection to her deceased relative, Zach.

Pot has been legal in Canada for years. Yet I never think of anyone lighting up at 11:30 in the morning. Apparently, I don't live in the real world.

I'm on pause for a moment. But then rebound—my only choice is to fight fire with fire.

'What I want to know is what Rolinda Smith has to do with a man by the name of Philippe Jean. From Martinique. Visiting Saint-Pierre and Miquelon.'

Her aggression has taken a direct hit. Her neck retreats into her shoulders.

She slams the door in my face.

We stand there, vaguely waiting for something more to transpire.

Nothing does. Unless you count a sharp click, the distinct sound of the door being locked.

'So much for that,' says Mae.

I could add that Rolinda Smith is definitely askew. That she's hiding something, absolutely. Whatever the hell that something is.

There's nothing more to be done at this point to find out. A composed, unflinching return to the car is the expedient option.

We pull out of the driveway and head along the road until we're out of sight of the Smith lair. We park and look at each other.

Now what?

It's at moments like this that I wish I had cop credentials. To wave in her face and hit her with the fact that I'd be back before the day is over with a bloody search warrant. Put that in your bong and smoke it.

What I do have is an iron-gut determination to get to the bottom of just what in the hell's name has gone on with Rolinda Smith. And, more to the point, her son, the convicted drug smuggler. By the smell of it, he comes by his predilection for dope naturally. Like mother, like son.

'One more stop,' I tell Mae, 'before we head to St. John's. I'm not sure where it will get us. Let's hope it's somewhere worthwhile.'

Optimistic. Yet realistic. We're talking the RCMP.

I've calmed myself to the point of being both optimistic *and* level-headed. Mae pats me on the leg as I restart the car. *And*, I will add, well-grounded.

With two thumbs projecting up from the steering wheel, I drive away. It takes an hour to reach Marystown. Shortly after one o'clock we're walking up to the front entrance of the spanking new RCMP detachment on McGettigan Boulevard. A fresh vibe permeates the air.

The RCMP have consolidated their presence on the Burin Peninsula to a single detachment. Closing out the other offices was controversial at the time, but you have to think the higher-ups knew what they were doing. A modern, up-to-date complex staffed with an arsenal of expertly trained Mounties is bound to instill confidence in a general populace needing protection from the unsavoury elements that lurk in the dark corners of the peninsula.

'Build it and they will come,' I quip as we near the intercom that will allow us to state our business and gain access to the inside.

'May I help you?' The charming female voice of the receptionist emerges from the speaker.

I state our names. 'We would like to speak to the officer in charge of the detachment concerning Zach Russell of Lamaline, who, as he is likely aware, died under suspicious circumstances on Saint-Pierre.'

'That would be Staff Sergeant *Candace* Windermere. One moment please.'

Surprising. Female and with a name that sounds rather . . . well, genteel. Mae is pleased, yet equally intrigued. We're on standby, eyebrows now relaxed.

In short order there's a sharp, efficient buzz. I hold the door open for Mae and soon we're both inside, single-minded and eager. There's a brief exchange with the receptionist before we're led along a pristine corridor to an open door.

'Come in.' The officer holds out her hand and introduces herself. We follow suit.

Staff Sergeant Candace Windermere is on the youthful side of middle age. Her brown hair is short and layered, with blonde highlights, in a style that I think is termed "sassy." (Or used to be, at least, back in the day.)

Her handshake tells me there is more muscle where that came from. Her smile is exact, though she is by no means unfriendly. It appears her years in the force have taught her to maintain a distance on first meeting. Criminal investigation demands caution, as we both know.

'Please take a seat.' She is quick to the business at hand. 'You are here under the assumption that this detachment is working with the office of *la gendarmerie* in Saint-Pierre on the investigation into the death of Zach Russell of Lamaline. Is this correct?'

'Yes.'

'Before going any further, however, I will need to know more about who it is I'm speaking with. What are your backgrounds? And what exactly is your involvement in the situation regarding the deceased?'

Make that cautious and efficient. The officer listens for the next few minutes. At the mention of finding the body, something clicks. Tremblay would have told her about us, although possibly not mentioned our names.

'I see. My condolences to you both.'

And when I think I've said enough, her response is equally brief. 'Private investigator. I see.'

Her name is a misnomer. Candace Windermere is very far from genteel. Her people skills could use a little fine-tuning, but there it is, we're in no position to be anything but forthcoming.

'What exactly have you observed, Mr. Synard, that you think would be of interest to the RCMP?'

Judging by her tone, her expectations are low.

'You're familiar with Johnny Smith, resident of Lamaline?'

A sudden uptake of interest, guardedly articulated. 'Yes.'

And we go from there. The staff sergeant, of course, knows a great deal about the man in question. And, as it turns out, his mother. She is not about to divulge it all, and what she does say comes with unequivocal focus on how the duo connects to the investigation.

I relate all I have discovered about Johnny and Rolinda, which, although it doesn't amount to a great deal, boosts the eagerness on the officer's part to know more about what we can offer the investigation.

'What can you tell me about this Philippe Jean?'

That, too, is limited. And I'm left with impression that, although the cops on Saint-Pierre might have mentioned Johnny Smith to her, they certainly haven't said anything about Philippe Jean.

'The *gendarmerie* has been informed about the link between Smith and Jean,' Mae tells her. Calling them by their surnames makes us sound like we mean business.

Even so, for the moment Staff Sergeant Windermere keeps her thoughts about Philippe Jean to herself. She's got to be considering why Tremblay hadn't mentioned the guy. Because he's a citizen of France, the colonel's turf? I doubt it. It's more likely because the good colonel figures he is of no importance to the case.

I elaborate about Philippe Jean's time in Newfoundland prior to going to Saint-Pierre. It stirs the pot further. The officer tries her best not to show it, but it looks to me like she's hooked into finding out more.

'Just why was weedhead Rolinda Smith from Lamaline on the phone to Saint-Pierre asking about fashion designer Philippe Jean from Martinique?' A strategic manoeuvre on my part.

'Leave it with me.' She says no more.

She doesn't have to. The picture is already in my head. Before the day is out she and a second uniformed officer will board a fully loaded squad car and hit the road for the Smith house in Lamaline. A shit-baked, pot-smoking mother will answer the door. She'll be far from crude. And not for a fraction of a second will she consider jerking her carcass back inside and slamming the door in their faces.

How I wish I could be there to witness it. Unfortunately, it's not RCMP protocol to have anyone tag along out of interest. Staff Sergeant Windermere is expecting us to be on the road in the other direction. 'You have a four-hour drive ahead of you.'

We decide to take the hint. I stand up, if slowly and with some semblance of indecision. 'I expect we'll be in touch,' I tell her.

'Of course.'

She's not entirely convincing. I hesitate, but better safe than sorry. I will have to bring out my trump card.

'I'll be speaking with Inspector Bowmore. She'll also keep me posted.'

That would be Inspector Ailsa Bowmore, provincial head of the Criminal Investigation Unit at RCMP headquarters in St. John's. Staff Sergeant Windermere is, shall we say, a little disconcerted. I try not to look like I notice.

'We've worked together on other cases,' I tell her. 'She's a friend, from way back.' (Somewhat more than a friend at one point, but that's pre-Mae and well in the past, and staying there.) 'We're in regular contact.' Not entirely true, but it's been no more than a few months since we last spoke.

'I see,' responds the officer.

Cautious and professionally assertive. Like you would.

We're again on the highway, heading back up The Boot. It's hard to think it's been less than a week since we so innocently cruised down it.

'So much has played out.'

'So much yet to take the stage,' Mae says.

'Always the way.'

If we're prone to clichés it's because we're tired. All that

French. Exhausting. God knows I tried. I gave it my best shot, but no question, it's a relief to be back on home turf.

Mae is tired for other reasons. It was meant to be a relaxing hiatus from all the drama of running her business. Instead, she walked into another murder scene. No wonder she's dozed off.

We've made it as far as Goobies and have just turned onto the Trans-Canada when Mae wakes up.'Want me to drive?' she asks, not missing a beat, as if she's not been comatose all this time.

'Sure.' I could use the break. Besides, Morris the Moose beckons.

We turn again and park the car just next to the favoured beast. There is something reassuring about the statue. Life might have its traumas, but the ungulate Morris still stands, unperturbed.

We exit the car and stretch, change drivers and press on.

'Once we get home,' I tell Mae, 'you should try to put all this out of your mind. You need some downtime.'

'It won't be that simple.'

'No really, I can take it from here.' Just being considerate.

She apparently doesn't see it that way. 'Are you saying you'd rather go it alone?'

'What I'm saying is you have more than enough to deal with at the shop.'

'Isn't that for me to decide?' Calm but assertive.

I can't win for losing. 'Trying to being helpful, that's all.'

I brace myself for more.

What I get is silence. I dare not say anything.

It goes on for far too long. We've reached Whitbourne, less than a hundred kilometres left to drive.

A deep, inaudible breath. 'I'm sorry if I offended you.' I could say more, like if I did, it was entirely unintentional. I hold back. The less she has to work with the better.

'I've been thinking.'

She's had plenty of time to do that. Another deep, inaudible intake.

'I've been thinking you should go to Martinique and track down Philippe Jean.'

Out of nowhere. Don't know whether I should be thankful or suspicious.

What's she really saying? . . . Okay, you want to take charge, do it, show what you're made of, put me out of the picture, big time.

I can handle this. 'Possibly.'

'Let's be realistic. It's the only way you're going to get the answers you're looking for.'

'Big bucks.'

'Brian is good for it.'

Possibly. This time unvoiced.

'Besides,' she adds, 'All that sand and sun. You could use the downtime.'

She glances at me. Not exactly a smile. But not a smirk. Overall, it feels like a compromise, I think.

Mae and I have been considering moving in together. I get the feeling that will likely be put on hold.

A tidy, affectionate parting on the Gower Street sidewalk and now she's behind closed doors in her own home. We both still need space it seems.

Looks like that space could possibly amount to roughly four thousand kilometres. As the crow flies. Or longer, if you take into account I would have to fly to Montreal before connecting to Martinique.

Air fare plus accommodation plus meals—like I said, big bucks. Would the Russells foot the bill? Even if they did, would it be worth it? I couldn't contact Philippe Jean beforehand in case he'd decide to fly the coop. What if I get there and I can't track him down? What then?

All critical questions for later. Right now I have to pick up Gaffer and deal with the countless questions that Samantha is sure to have about Nick and what's gone on over the last few days.

I ring the bell and Gaffer comes running, barking up a storm. The master has returned. Let the canine lickfest begin.

You've got to love it. No restraint. No underlying emotion. Just barrelling into you, full-on, out-and-out affection.

When he's finally done licking, I stand back up, prepared to take on the barrage. I texted Samantha in advance so her aim should be straight and to the point.

She's been in regular contact with me, and with Nick of course. Regardless, I shouldn't fault the urgency in a mother's voice.

'I want to know everything that happened. From the very beginning.'

As if repeating what I've already told her over the phone will be of benefit. Nevertheless, I comply. It takes time. Not long into it, Frederick—the live-in—appears. He stands silently behind Samantha, equally attentive to the narrative. I assure them that Nick will be okay, convinced as I am (fingers crossed) that he's reached a level of stability that will get him through the remainder of the term.

Samantha has her doubts. 'On Saturday we're heading to Saint-Pierre to see him.'

I'm not surprised. 'Perfect.' An overstatement, but Nick will appreciate seeing his mother. And Frederick, possibly.

When I get to today's drama in Lamaline and Marystown, interest in the story peaks. New particulars leave them anxious to know more.

'Come in and sit down,' Frederick says. 'I'll pour you a Scotch. Sounds like you could use it.'

Frederick and I have come a long way. There was a time when just the sight of him was enough to drive me round the bend, to put it mildly. Within a few months of the divorce there he was, showing up like nobody's business. Except mine—him getting to spend more time with Nick than I did. On top of the fact he's a pumped-up police inspector with the Royal Newfoundland Constabulary and every time I take on an investigation, there he is, large as life.

So Nick grew up. The situation mellowed over time, to the point Frederick is now offering me Ardbeg in a Glencairn glass. He doesn't even like peaty Scotch. A major step beyond reconciliation. He appreciates what I've been going through with Nick.

What was meant to be a quick visit to pick up Gaffer turns into communion with the amorous couple, all of a sudden keenly focused on the fact that I'm deep into the dirt of the investigation to find out how Nick's friend ended up dead.

Frederick, the cop, is particularly intent. 'This Johnny has a police record,' he says. Which is his way of letting me know that for him the details of his criminal background are only a few computer clicks away.

Not only that but Frederick has what he considers "a reasonably good friend" among the twenty-seven *gendarmes* on Saint-Pierre and Miquelon. Apparently the guy brings his tracker dog into St. John's for training exercises with the RNC dogs.

Frederick doesn't go beyond that. He's waiting for word from me. He knows his involvement in what I'm about is still a sensitive issue. Nevertheless, the Ardbeg speaks volumes.

'Have a look at his record,' I tell him. 'If there's something you think I should be aware of, fill me in. As for the guy with the dog, let's wait and see how far I get with his boss.'

Pause. 'If that's the way you want it.'

Frederick is no doubt wondering why I'm not latching onto the fact that cop-to-cop chitchat would likely be far more productive than civilian me on the phone to Colonel Tremblay.

For now I'll hang on to my independence. There might come a time when I'll need Frederick to do more than check his computer screen, but we're not there yet.

Let's leave that ace up my sleeve for now. Flying solo is the preferred option, which, when I think about it, is exactly what I will be doing to make the move on the elusive fashion designer.

'I figure I might just head to Martinique. My next step is to track down Philippe Jean.'

Samantha is taken aback, of course, by the nonchalance, but also by the fact that in her mind it doesn't add up. International travel is not a match for my financial status.

Before she asks I tell her, 'It's in the budget.'

That is, if Brian and Lisa approve. I need not go there.

'The sun and sand are secondary,' I add. 'It's all about the manhunt.'

Frederick looks underwhelmed. In an earlier time I might have said cynical. Not now, not knowing as he does that I've proven myself more than capable over the course of past investigations/manhunts.

'Be careful,' he says. 'You'll be in a foreign country. Play by their rules.'

I could point out that I have the experience of Saint-Pierre and Miquelon under my belt. I decide instead to let him have this one, with a grain of salt. 'I will.'

By the time we part company a framework has been established. We'll definitely keep in touch, each on a visit to our own *collectivité territoriale.*

Two French islands, both relatively small. Population—Martinique: 350,000, Saint-Pierre and Miquelon: 6,000. Average daytime temperature in October—Martinique: 27°C, Saint-Pierre: 9°C. Sandy beaches—Martinique: 120 . . .

Merely preparing myself for the differences. Gloating would be déclassé.

Gaffer consumes the rest of my waking hours. The mutt is excited beyond barks to be back in his own space. He sniffs about, reacquainting himself with every well-known corner. Then revels in a meal only his master is willing to take time to prepare, followed by his all-time special treat—frozen yoghurt in a dog-size cone. He does eventually relax and curl up next to me in the comfy chair. Unconditional love is my reward.

He lies contentedly listening to anything I say, with no urge to voice an opposing opinion. Just letting me be me, sipping the *Eddu Brocéliande* I picked up in Saint-Pierre, the dog noting just how much I'm enjoying it. 'Must be the buckwheat, Gaffer. *Superbe*.'

In the morning I'm still thinking about the whisky. I sit up in bed, Gaffer stretched out nearby. I'm researching what book I might pair it with for my whisky blog, *Distill My Reading Heart*. The blog is a hobby, in some eyes unconventional perhaps. Beloved by a select group.

It's not exactly rocking the internet, but it has its faithful followers. A pensive lot that appreciates the combination of the literary and the drinkworthy. One such individual recently left a comment saying, "Keep it up. I'm loving what you do."

Right on, pal. You and your mates make it all worthwhile. That said, what I have to do now is come up with a book to complement the *Eddu*. I'm of course thinking something French, something off the beaten track, something that goes against the grain.

It is still on my mind over coffee. At the same time, I'm coming to grips with an expansion of my waistline due to French pastry consumption. (It was worth it.) I unceremoniously retreat to the Intermittent Fasting regime, meaning nothing but black coffee until eleven.

The caffeine at least fires the brain cells to the point I've built up the courage to phone Brian in Lamaline.

'Good morning. It's Sebastian. Sorry to be calling so early.'

'Just finished up the last sausage. I'm good.'

Does nothing for his midsection for sure. But I can't be distracted.

I lay out the possibility of flying to Martinique, with what I think is a reasoned take on the need to confront Philippe Jean directly. 'The cops on Saint-Pierre are showing no interest in pursuing the guy, even though, to my mind, he's absolutely key to what happened.'

Brian, after a private one-on-one with Lisa, is not entirely convinced. 'Say he turns on you, hauls out a knife? Then you're up shit creek.'

He's been watching too much TV. But arguing won't get me anywhere. 'I'll have insurance.'

'Say he aims for more than your leg.'

Neither will shock tactics do him any good. 'I can be very quick on my feet.'

In the end he realizes I mean business. Combined with his determination to find out what truly happened, he pauses, then confers with Lisa once more before coming back on the line. 'Keep your receipts. And just so we're clear, we won't be covering hospital bills.'

'Thanks for trusting in me.' Keeping it buoyant.

Lisa's voice stretches to reach the phone. 'You might be our only hope.'

'You have my word that I won't be coming back empty-handed.' Unflinchingly buoyant.

On that note the call ends. As I slip my phone in my pocket, reality strikes.

No more blowing hot and cold—I'm about to fly off to the Caribbean.

In the meantime, I bundle up and take Gaffer for a walk. I'm not long back when I get a text from Frederick, in his official capacity as Inspector Olsen. The man is known for not wasting time.

–Served twelve months of an eighteen-month sentence for dealing cocaine. First offense. Released August 12.

Sounds like he wasn't caught with a big stash, jail time a warning to get his act together. Get caught a second time, and he could be behind bars for years.

–Thanks for this.

–I could call the detachment in Marystown to get an update.

That I'll deal with myself.

–Thanks for the offer. Hold off for now.

Besides which I have the option of brainstorming with someone who's a step up from Olsen.

I'll admit that I'm not exactly sure what I'll say to her. I'll need to judge her mood.

She's a busy woman. When I finally get Inspector Bowmore on the line, it's clear she's on a tight agenda.

'Hello, Sebastian. How are you?'

'Fine. And yourself?'

'Fine. What can I do for you?' She would normally ask about Nick. Which I was counting on as a lead-in.

'Perhaps this is not a good time. Should I call back?'

'Is it urgent?'

'It's about the death of the MUN student in Saint-Pierre. Nick was in his class.'

Her time allotment suddenly expands. 'Is Nick all right?'

'Traumatized, but getting over it. Unfortunately, he was with us when Mae and I discovered the body.'

The allotment disappears altogether. 'Good God, Sebastian, I hadn't realized who it was. It must have been awful.'

'I've seen worse. As you will recall.'

'But still.'

'Absolutely. Nick and the young man were beginning a relationship.'

It takes a few moments for her to absorb it.

In the meantime I add, 'My investigation is deep into the details.'

She's anything but surprised. Although she does not raise the point, our past histories with other cases would have instilled a solid measure of confidence that I know what I'm about.

'I've been in regular contact with the detachment in Marystown of course,' she says, 'and with the *gendarmerie* on Saint-Pierre.'

Neither of which, it seems, has seen any reason to mention me. That would be admitting that someone other than their well-salaried selves had discovered anything important to the case.

'Did they happen to refer to a person by the name of Philippe Jean?'

'That name doesn't ring a bell.'

I proceed to ring it for her. Concluding with the fact that I'm about to fly off to track the guy down.

'Sebastian, it's a foreign country.'

As if I haven't heard that before.

'I suggest the first thing you do when you get there is contact the local police and explain the situation. If they need verification you're legitimate, I can do that. It's important you play by their rules.'

Yes, a distinct echo. 'I'll be sure to keep that in mind, as I do all such advice.' If there's a mild note of sarcasm, it's completely incidental.

'It's likely your accreditation might not hold up.'

More than likely. But let's keep that to one side.

My reason for contacting Inspector Bowmore (under these circumstances I hesitate to call her Ailsa) was to make sure she has me on her radar. I'm now certain that my involvement with the case will find its way into any future discussions she undertakes with comrades Windermere and Tremblay. It will act as a needed boost to my profile.

Mission accomplished. 'I'll keep you posted on whatever transpires in Martinique.'

'Yes, absolutely.'

Music to my ears. Confirmation that I now have a single, direct, and favourable channel to the police sector of the investigation.

'And, Sebastian . . .'

'Yes, Ailsa . . .'

'Be careful. I wouldn't want anything to happen to you.'

A pause. One tinged with emotional residue.

We go our separate ways, but there's a lift in knowing that our once intimate relationship has had lasting positive effects.

I time the call to Nick to coincide with his noon break. His morning classes have ended and I catch him as he's walking back to Emmeline's for lunch.

'Just a minute.' I hear other voices fade away. He's letting his friends go ahead before he chats with me.

'You're good?' I ask.

'Yeah, pretty good. Considering.'

Not sounding quite as positive as I had hoped. But no point in going there, better to keep it upbeat. 'I'm heading off to Martinique.'

He's caught unawares. With his focus shifted, it doesn't take long to get him up to speed on the rationale for the journey south.

'Really? Sounds fraught to me.'

Fraught? Clearly his English hasn't suffered any in Saint-Pierre.

'You mean *dangereux*.' Keeping things on an even keel.

Did I detect the hint of a chuckle? Hardly perceptible. But promising. Yes.

'I'll be careful. I don't think of Philippe Jean as hostile necessarily. He may have flown out of Saint-Pierre without knowing what happened. He may not even realize he's holding information about Johnny Smith that could prove useful.'

'In that case, why not just call him?'

'In an investigation, one-on-one is always preferable.'

'Just in case he's hiding something. And if he is, and doesn't want you to know that, then the encounter is potentially fraught.'

Potentially fraught is no less a caution than fraught.

I need to draw a line. 'Nick, I promise I'll be careful. Trust me, I won't do anything foolish.'

'Not intentionally at least.'

I bite my tongue. I let him have the last word.

Nevertheless, there it is, end of that exchange. Time to move to other matters.

'Anything new on your end? Emmeline have any luck?'

'Hold for a minute. I've just arrived back at the house.'

Presumably he's checking with Emmeline for an update. I don't hold out much hope.

At that point I hear an eager stream of French. It escapes me entirely. There are short interjections from Nick, but nothing that slows down the response. Finally it reaches an end and Nick is back on the line to me.

'Did you get any of that?'

I did catch my own name a couple of times, but for the sake of expediency I respond, 'Not really.'

'Emmeline thinks she might be on to something. Apparently there's one woman who grew up on the Burin Peninsula who's married and living on the *route du Cap aux Basques*, in one of those big houses you would have noticed when you hiked to *la pointe du Diamant*. Emmeline knows someone who does housecleaning there. A bit of a long shot maybe but she's waiting to hear back from her friend.'

'I *do* remember those houses. I can't get too excited at this point, but it sounds like there's reason for optimism.' Putting a positive spin on it, hopefully one that's justified.

'I'll keep you posted,' Nick says, with what I take to be enthusiasm.

The news from Emmeline has put a dent in his melancholy, in itself a big plus. 'You're as anxious as I am to see where this leads. Pass along my thanks to your very helpful *mère française*.'

I put the phone on speaker and turn it toward Gaffer. He yelps his approval.

'Hey, Gaffer. It's Nick. How you doin', buddy?'

Gaffer yelps again, and again. The two have their moment. Yet another reason for optimism.

'Mom arrives tomorrow,' Nick says just before we're about to disconnect.

'So she does. She's anxious to see you.'

'We're having dinner at Les P'tits Graviers.'

'Nice.'

'Mom and Fred.'

It still strikes a nerve when he calls him Fred. I push past it. 'Nice.'

A momentary gap in the conversation. Nothing "fraught." Samantha and Olsen will be a good distraction for him.

'I better get going. I'll soon have to dig out the sunscreen.'

'Play it safe, Dad.'

'As a way of saving my own skin? I have no intention of getting burned.'

I'm thinking he might be smiling as we hang up.

I'll be honest. As much as I love the city where I live, its weather is often the pits. Days on end of what we grudgingly call RDF—rain, drizzle, and fog. And to add insult to injury—habitual wind. In fact, St. John's has the lamentable distinction of being the windiest city in the whole of Canada.

Of course, there's good reason for it—we're on an island stuck out in the North Atlantic, where the cold Labrador Current confronts the balmy Gulf Stream. (The Labrador Current wins every time.) And, yes, our whereabouts are also why we get stunningly beautiful icebergs drifting past our shores. But that, my friends, is inadequate compensation.

Yet, what can we do but learn to live with it, or escape. In my case—escape, unexpectedly.

'Current weather in Fort-de-France—sunny and 31°C.'

'You'll enjoy that,' responds Mae.

We're sitting across from each other at The Duke of Duckworth, consuming their famous fish and chips. Outside it's raining. With gusts hitting 40 km/h.

'I doubt if you'll get fish as tasty as this in Martinique,' she notes.

'Possibly.' I should avoid playing up the fact that I'm catching a flight in the morning to Montreal and connecting to another that will see me arrive in Martinique in (glancing at my phone) less than twenty hours from now. I overcome the temptation by filling my mouth with a forkful of french fries.

I reposition our conversation to the fact that tomorrow Samantha and Frederick will be on their way to Saint-Pierre. 'Nick will have plenty to keep him busy. Hopefully it will keep his mind off what happened to Zach.'

'I doubt that will happen. But she'll help him deal with it.'

You could look at it that way.

'Mothers and sons have a special relationship. I'm thinking she'll work with him to find a perspective to help him through it.'

I don't say anything. I'm not particularly happy with that. And I don't hide it well.

'I'm not saying you and Nick don't also have a special relationship. You're great together. But you two communicate on a different level. It's just as important, but it's not the same. Father to son is different. Man to man is different.'

This coming from a woman who has one child, a daughter.

She can see she's touched a nerve. I'm not about to overreact, but let's be fair—Nick and I have something more than a "special relationship," whatever that means. We understand each other, we support each other, we have all the time in the world for each other. What the heck is she going on about? Is she saying that his mother can be more of a help to him than I can?

I don't ask. I sit there and eat my meal.

'I'm sorry.'

It seems she's been saying that a lot lately.

'It's just my interpretation. I don't mean anything by it. Parents each have their own strengths.' She pauses. 'Life is complicated.'

She got that bloody well right.

Calm down, Sebastian. You're on the verge. Don't say something you'll regret. This woman means a lot to you.

Eat your meal. Drink your beer. Look like you're okay.

'Life *is* complicated. You got that right.'

HUIT

31°C AND RAINING.

But heat is heat. As I exit the Air Canada flight at Martinique Aimé Césaire International Airport I note that in the city of my departure it is at this moment partially sunny and, get this, 10°C.

Fortunately, they sell umbrellas at the airport. The driver grabs my carry-on and opens the cab door and soon I'm inside looking out as the rain lashes the sunroof.

We're headed to Les Trois-Îlets, a *commune* of Martinique, and to the smallest of its seaside villages, L'Anse à l'Âne. Which sounds so much better in the French than in translation—Donkey Cove if you're polite, Jackass Cove if you're not.

The pronunciation I have down pat thanks to YouTube. Unfortunately, it's so spot-on that the driver thinks my French is better than his English.

'*Très belle plage, pas trop fréquentée.*'

The first half I know. Great beach. And I take a stab at the second half. 'Not many people.'

'*Exactement. Pas beaucoup de touristes.*'

Yes, that's exactly why I picked it. Great beach, but not overrun with tourists.

Plus, it has a quick shuttle ferry to nearby Fort-de-France, the island's capital. And, most important of all, it's within walking distance of La Pointe du Bout, the commercial tourist mecca of Les Trois-Îlets, with Martinique's largest concentration of shops, including one known as La Boutique de Philippe. (Complete with a Facebook page that looks dead on the money.)

By the time we arrive at the Airbnb, the rain has abruptly stopped. I like this—no intermittent drizzle and nothing resembling fog. Cloud-covered but the temperature stuck at 31°.

'*Bonne chance!*' says the departing driver, after I've added a generous tip from the small wad of euros I secured from my bank before leaving home.

Everything according to plan, including adequate, mid-scale accommodation, at a ten-minute walk from the beach. Which I head straight for, having hurriedly pared down to swim shorts, T-shirt, and sandals.

Unreal! In a nutshell—French Caribbean heaven. I can get pumped by the sight of a stretch of white sand in Newfoundland, but let's face it, what I'm now walking on barefoot is wantonly warm, a sensation that continues when these same feet are submerged in the seawater that is lapping lovingly to shore. All a small part of the broad expanse of sand that rings the inlet, here and there punctuated by palm trees and a scattering of bars and restaurants. Palm trees that, when the sun is out, must give much-needed shade while you down yet another frosted cocktail. How friggin' awesome is this.

I haven't enveloped myself in such a decadent body of water in a very long time. I freestyle my way parallel to the shore, a man intoxicated by the briny sweep over a body too long constricted by weather and clothes. Not only that—it's shedding years off me. If I didn't know better, I could be friggin' twenty-something.

When I run out of muscle power I'm opposite one of the beachside bars, the kind you always see pictured, with the thatched umbrellas woven from palm leaves. How cliché, how perfect.

I jog along the beach, back to where I had discarded the T-shirt and sandals. By the time I reach them I'm reasonably dry, dry enough at least that when I make it back to the beach bar, the T-shirt only clings to me in a few inconspicuous places. From the pocket of the shorts I retrieve a waterproof pouch holding my phone and credit card, as I sink breezily into a beach chair and under a thatched umbrella.

A glance around leaves me wondering why the beach bar has only one other person like myself who feels deserving of this utopia. True, at this hour there is no need for the umbrella, the clouds having failed to drift away.

'Where's everyone?' I ask Céline, the young woman who arrives to take my order, her smallish name tag embellishing a skimpy top. '*Il n'y a personne.*'

'*C'est la saison des pluies.*'

'*Des pluies?*'

She stretches one hand skyward and draws it down, doing that wriggly thing with her fingers.

I see. And almost on cue there is a clap of thunder.

There's something to be said for sitting under a thatched umbrella drinking first a rum-rich *Ti'punch*, the signature cocktail of Martinique, followed by a frothy glass of the local BAM Pale Ale, while the sky has opened up and the rain spills relentlessly around you. The thing to be said is that it's still +30°C with not a draft of wind. Plus, the cocktail packs an extraordinary punch. And the beer is brilliant. I, for one, am not the least surprised when my phone reveals that it won a gold medal at *Le Concours Général Agricole* in Paris three years ago.

Céline is sitting idly on a stool inside the shelter of the bar, chatting with the bartender. They look roughly the same age. They share a joke with a notable lack of restraint. The black tank top partially covering the fellow's brawn displays a single word—*flâneur.*

Intriguing. Google solves the mystery, to some extent. It's one of those French words that doesn't translate well into English. But I get the idea—a wanderer, an idler, a dude who strolls about, wallowing in new encounters.

Oh, to be that young again. Knowing what I know now.

A useless lament, and not one to brood over even as I look at the fellow with envy, his eyes following Céline's provocative stride as she makes her way to me now that the rain has let up.

'*Une autre bière, monsieur?*'

I think not. It's best if I get myself in gear to return to the Airbnb, change my clothes, send off a few emails, then go in search of a restaurant where I can have a quiet dinner, alas, by myself.

I had been skeptical of the mosquito netting, but when I wake up and find I'm scratching only one bite I'm thankful. And thankful, too, that the host has stocked the fridge with a few breakfast items, including guava juice and a couple of black sausage links labelled *boudin créole.*

Now here's a fun way to start the day, whipping up a Caribbean breakfast in your underwear while still scratching that one bite. The host has even attached a note with what could be instructions on how to cook the sausage in the microwave. My phone translation app reveals it only takes three minutes per link on high. Time enough to get into a pair of spiffy walking shorts, polo shirt, and running shoes.

The *boudin créole* is a treat and a half, rather spicy, as I like my sausages. With the guava juice, followed by a cup of Ti'Kafé coffee, made with island-grown beans.

It all makes me feel authentically *Martiniquais*, emboldening the dude for the critical day ahead. A half-hour later I step out into morning sunshine, backpack secure—repository for sunscreen, water bottle, and (merely playing it safe) umbrella.

First scheduled stop—La Boutique de Philippe. Keeping my financial backers in mind, I review the three options for getting there. Taxi—not in the budget. Ferry to Fort-de-France, then wait to connect to the ferry to La Pointe du Bout—considerably cheaper, but time-consuming. Or the cost-free trail through the woods to L'Anse Mitan, from where it's a short jaunt to the final destination.

Needing to release some of that morning muscular tension, I choose the healthy option. So, let's make this happen.

The trail looks to be not much frequented, as expected. It's rough in places (also as expected, having viewed the photos online), requiring some nimble footwork over exposed tree roots. The elevation gain is sizable, but then you always know you have to come down again to reach sea level. All good over the forty or so minutes it takes to reach the wider world once again.

I emerge on the streets of L'Anse Mitan, taking the one that runs parallel to its beach, a stretch of white sand much longer than that of L'Anse à l'Âne, and with an offshore that provides anchorage for spiffier yachts. I'd say the whole town is a happening place at the height of the tourist season, dotted as it is with multi-storey hotels and apartment buildings that ascend into the hills beyond the shoreline. I'd say robustly prosperous, in the mass-market sense.

But, unlike L'Anse à l'Âne, lacking rustic charm. It doesn't quite do it for me. I'd give it seven out of ten.

Time to take another slug of water and keep going. It's ten more minutes to La Pointe du Bout.

If L'Anse Mitan didn't float my boat, La Pointe du Bout sinks it.

Its marina unnerves me. All those yachts lined up, row after row. I'm not used to being so blatantly confronted by how the other half lives. And no, it doesn't amount to envy. I do respect their wealth. Either they inherited well or worked like hell to reach this level of conspicuous consumption.

The verdict is reinforced when I enter the outdoor shopping mall where La Boutique de Philippe is located. The mall, according to the arching sign over its entrance, has been named Village Créole.

To my reading of history, the word "*créole*" implies colonization and the lower end of the economic ladder. I look at the jazzy signage and I'm thinking the name of the mall lacks context.

Okay, I'm an outsider, so I'll keep my thoughts to myself. Which doesn't stop me from having a gut feeling there's something askew about this collection of cute, pastel-painted boutiques with gingerbread gable trim.

Once I start walking around, the dramatic monologue is replaced by a starker reality. There it is—La Boutique de Philippe.

And here I am—pretty sure I'm about to lay eyes on the man I figure must know a hell of a lot about what led to the turmoil of the past week.

I didn't come all this way to hesitate at the entrance. The PI genes kick in unceremoniously.

I'm faced with a young man, Caucasian, if well-tanned. Clearly not Philippe Jean.

'Good morning, *monsieur. Merci* for coming in. Relax, *monsieur, prenez votre temps*, look around, *s'il vous plaît*. If you need help, *mon nom est Grégoire*.'

A salesman who has both bases covered. The shopping mall obviously attracts a lot of foreigners.

'*Dankeschön.*' Not to be outdone.

'*Guten Tag.*'

I happen to know "thank you" in Latvian, but I think better of it.

'I'm from Canada. It's bilingual, as you might know. I'm good with English, thanks.'

'Wonderful. Escaping the snow?'

'Not quite. A couple of months yet.' I forgive him and move about the shop. Fortunately for me, I'm his only customer.

I don't want to give him the impression that I'm actually not interested in buying anything, but rather that I'm loaded, and could at any minute lay hold of a pricey few items and pile them on the checkout counter.

I move intently about the shop. And then, in less than thirty seconds I silently but unequivocally declare yes! There's absolutely no doubt—I'm inside the retail premises of one Philippe Jean.

There, on prominent display, is the running cap worn by Liam in Rencontre East. And just beyond it the neck gaiter/scrunchie worn by the museum attendant in Grand Bank.

Petty items compared to the chic collection of casual clothes and beachwear that fills the shop. I discreetly flip the price tags of what I expect are costlier pieces, confirming just how big a hit my credit card would take.

And then my eyes strike, in a more tropical fabric, the same style of swim shorts Zach Russell was wearing when he was found dead among the seaweed of Île aux Marins.

Enough of this. I came here for a reason. Cut to the chase.

'Will Philippe be in the shop today? I have business with him.' Sounding as if we already know each other. Sounding as if I'm a prospective wholesale client.

In Grégoire's eyes I was about to pluck something off a rack and ask to try it on. My question throws him off his sales trajectory.

He struggles for an answer. '*Oui.* Sorry, yes, I think so.'

'Soon?'

'He often comes in this time of the day. After he stops for coffee.'

'Where? Where does he stop for coffee?'

'Really, *monsieur*, I'm not sure . . .' He's second-guessing who I might be.

'This is urgent.'

'Relax, *monsieur, prenez votre temps*, look around, *s'il vous plaît*.'

He's backtracking. He's not about to reveal where the elusive Philippe Jean stops on his way to work. I exit the shop and plant myself firmly under its awning. Grégoire remains inside, likely glaring out at me.

I wait. Long enough that I drop a text to Mae, reporting on what I've been up to for the last half-hour.

Strangely for her, she doesn't answer right away. Another waiting game.

Finally, several minutes later, a response.

–Sorry. I was with a customer. Are you being careful? He could be armed.

Of course he's not armed. We're in France. He's not walking around with a handgun stuck inside his waistband.

I see someone in the distance, heading my way. A flashy dresser.

–Sorry. Gotta go.

The closer he gets the more I know it must be him. The fellow has the nonchalant, yet self-asserting gait of a fashion designer. Plus, he's wearing the same jacket I had been checking out inside the shop. And a duplicate of Liam's running cap. He's a walking advertisement for *Philippe Jean. Couturier. Casual with Class. Les Trois-Îlets, Martinique.*

'*Bonjour*,' he says, no doubt thinking I'm a customer about to go inside.

'*Bonjour*. My name is Sebastian Synard.' Without missing a beat I add, 'I've just been in Saint-Pierre.'

The rhythm could potentially continue.

It doesn't. He's speechless.

He tries not to react as if it's an accusation. He reacts instead as if I'm some aggressive weirdo with a personal bit of information that is of no interest to him whatsoever. He moves past me and grips the door handle.

I issue a challenge. 'You know Saint-Pierre, *monsieur?*'

I'm not to be ignored. He looks back.

'I know Saint-Pierre in Martinique, *monsieur*. I know Mount Pelée, *monsieur*.' And with that he pulls open the door and disappears inside.

Not so friggin' quick, *monsieur*. I'm about to launch myself in pursuit of him.

But no, I'm struck by a better strategy. He's not going anywhere. Let him stew in the fact that his foray abroad has caught up with him. Let him stew knowing he's going to have to come up with something better than whatever the hell he just spouted.

He stews while I google "*mount puhlay* Martinique," expecting a dead end.

Mount Pelée. Okay, so autocorrect works between languages.

"In Martinique pyroclastic flows from Mount Pelée instantly destroyed the town of Saint-Pierre and its 30,000 inhabitants."

I should know this. Vesuvius, I know. Etna, I know. Saint Helens, I know.

If I did know Pelée, I'd know there is also a Saint-Pierre in Martinique. A town that has been rebuilt since the eruption of the volcano in 1902.

Still, what's it got to do with the Philippe Jean who last week turned up in Saint-Pierre in the friggin' North Atlantic?

Nothing. A diversionary tactic. A ploy.

Yes, not so damn quick, *monsieur.*

I swing open the door and step inside. I don't advance far before Grégoire is in my face, in tough guy mode that doesn't deliver. I look around the shop. No Philippe Jean.

Grégoire holds his ground. Beyond him is a door, to a back room I suspect.

An aging, heavily tanned, verbose couple enters the shop. Fresh off an oversized yacht by the look of it. Grégoire is rigid still, but in the end has no choice but to step aside to deal with them. He hisses in my ear before generating a smile for the moneyed would-be customers.

'You-all carry string bikinis?' asks the woman.

The image she's generated is a harsh distraction, given how poorly her vital statistics equate with the intended purchase. I turn away and press on toward the door.

I tactfully open it halfway and peer inside. Confronting me is a mess of bleach-tipped curls rising above a swivel office chair.

He swerves away from the computer screen, folds his arms, and stares in my direction. They say never judge a man by his clothes, but even so the tropical fish vibe lacks combativeness. I step inside and close the door.

He nods toward a vacant chair. I remove my backpack and oblige. I stare back.

'*Sébastien*, what can I do for you?'

Should I take it as an attempt to ingratiate himself to me? Not so fast. Let's keep it rigidly professional. Let's get to the crux of the matter and see how long his *Sébastien* holds up.

'I'm a private detective, contracted by the parents of Zach Russell to investigate his death.' After his initial lurch, I continue, a quick, unconstrained summary of the investigation and how it embroils him and his gallivanting about Saint-Pierre, not to mention the Burin Peninsula.

'You have come all the way from *Terre-Neuve?*'

If there was an English equivalent of Martinique I'd be tempted to fit it in.

'You have come all this way to sit in my office and accuse me of murder. Ridiculous.'

I ignore the slight to my profession. 'I'm not accusing you of murder.' In any case I would leave that to the police, if I ever did reach that conclusion.

'A *conspirateur* to murder then. Ridiculous.'

'I'm here for one reason, Philippe Jean. One reason only. I'm here for you to tell me everything that occurred from the moment you first laid eyes on Zach Russell. And from the moment you first laid eyes on Johnny Smith.'

It's time for the man to cough up the goods, instead of taking his own sweet time to deal with what just smacked him in the face.

'I came all this way for fucking details.' Not to put too fine a point on it.

His own sweet time grinds to a halt. 'I knew Zach Russell was dead. I was told. By someone in Saint-Pierre.'

'Monique at Impromptu?'

At the point Monique first got in touch she might not have known it was murder. Although eventually she would have, and been left wondering if the fashion designer to whom she had suggested a model was somehow messed up in it.

The fellow is taken aback, of course, that I know of his connection to Monique. It edges me toward the driver's seat.

'I didn't hear from her again.'

Either he's lying, or because I showed up in Martinique, he's assuming it was murder.

'She's keeping her distance.'

Suddenly he's hit with the conclusion that in the eyes of the people he met in Saint-Pierre he *is* a murder suspect. I double the hit. 'And what about Amélie Dubois, have you heard from her?'

'Fuck, man.'

I now fully occupy the driver's seat. 'Okay, let's get to it. Start with how you first came in contact with Zach Russell.'

'I was looking for a model. Monique arranged it. We met in her shop. We hit it off.'

'Hit it off.' I hesitate for a moment, not sure I want to know the answer. 'How?'

He looks straight at me. 'I could say that's none of your business.' He holds back before adding, 'I tell you, man—the answer is no. He had his lucky guy. He had no interest. As you say in English—full stop. Period.'

Now it's me who holds back. To take in the relief. Zach's attraction to Philippe Jean had to be playing on Nick's mind. This will be some solace at least.

'So you set a time for a photo shoot? Was there more than one?'

He turns back to his computer. Finds what he's looking for, then moves aside so I can see. It's a photograph of Zach in swim shorts, standing in the sand, posing against the multi-coloured fence at *la plage de Savoyard.* Self-assured, clearly enjoying the moment.

Philippe scrolls through several other photographs taken on the same beach, stopping at one that I assume he thought worked particularly well—more of Zach, less of the fence, sunlight catching the crests of waves lapping ashore, a sweep of rust-coloured grasses in the background. Definitely not the tropics.

He scrolls on—to the beach at Île aux Marins. I remember its thick, mounded clumps of green and yellow kelp.

And here is Zach stretched back, basking against the kelp's glistening fronds, looking ethereal, otherworldly almost. But with a slight, cheeky smile, as if it's all lighthearted play.

An endearing smile, painful to look at knowing what transpired in the hour that followed. An hour during most of which, Philippe Jean contends, he was nowhere near the young man.

'He decided to stay. Hang out. Go for a swim. He said he might call his guy and see if he wanted to take the ferry and join him.'

He didn't get to make the call.

'I paid Zach and said goodbye. That was the last we saw of each other. I took the next ferry back to Saint-Pierre. Two hours later I was on a flight to *Montréal*, man. And the next morning on a flight to Martinique.'

Which I have no reason to doubt. Pascal at the *auberge* confirmed he dropped him off at the airport. For now at least I'll take Philippe at his word.

Then there's the matter of Johnny Smith.

'We met at the bar. Le Rustique. That was all. Believe me, man, that was all.'

'Crap.'

I don't take my eyes off him. He squirms a bit, refolds his arms to keep them still.

'Johnny Smith spent a year in jail for smuggling cocaine. You were looking for the stuff. He had it.'

'I wasn't looking for cocaine.'

'Like hell you weren't.'

'Listen, Mr. *Synard* . . .'

'You listen. Zach Russell was murdered on Île aux Marins. You just admitted you were there with him on the morning it happened. Which makes you a suspect in the eyes of the cops. Unless you come clean and tell everything you know, you're going to find yourself on a plane back to Saint-Pierre seated next to a *gendarme*, with handcuffs chafing your fucking wrists.'

His squirming is decidedly more pronounced. 'Shit.'

'Exactly.'

He admits what I suspected all along. He and Johnny Smith left Le Rustique, went off someplace, and snorted a few lines of cocaine.

'But that was it! Shit!'

Emphatic, but unconvincing.

'Really? What did you talk about?'

'I don't remember.'

'Would you rather do your remembering under the lights of the *la gendarmerie* interrogation room in Saint-Pierre?'

His agitation gives off a glistening sweat. 'I don't fucking remember, man,' his words trailing off.

'Let me give your brain a boost. Did you talk about Zach Russell?'

He holds off as long as he can, until, finally, he gets a grip. 'Yes.'

'What did you say to him?'

'He knew I had hired Zach. I don't know how.'

'Was this before or after you did the photo shoot at *la plage de Savoyard?*'

'After.'

'And you told him where and when the second shoot was going to be?'

Some hesitation, not much. 'Yes.'

'Why?'

'You know, man, coke makes you talk a lot.'

'He asked you specifically?'

'He said something about someone who knew Zach. His brother, I think. Something about high school.'

'Nothing more? That was it?'

'I can't remember, man. For real. I can't remember.'

Do I believe him? I'm of two minds. 'Did you see each other again?'

'No!'

I'm only somewhat convinced. 'Is that what you'll tell the cops in Saint-Pierre? The lights will be pretty fuckin' bright.'

'I didn't see Johnny Smith again!' His emotions have had it. 'Just shut up, man, with this shit.'

The last thing I want is a blubbering fashion designer on my hands.

I won't get anything else out of him. Maybe there's nothing else to come out. Maybe he's done all he can to save his ass.

'I'll tell you what—let's say I believe you. For now. If your cocaine fog clears and you have a sudden flash of recollections, call me.'

I tear a page from my notebook and scratch down my number, and for good measure, my address in L'Anse à l'Âne should he prefer it man-to-man.

'To be clear, the police in Newfoundland know exactly where I am and who I've come here to see.' Just in case he thinks there's a way to shut me up, permanently.

When I stand up he remains glued to the office chair. It's not a fond farewell.

I open the door and exit, shutting it quickly behind me.

In time to catch the yachting couple at the counter, credit card in motion.

'A little tight, but I like 'em tight,' she says.

I can only imagine. Also on the counter is a Speedo-cut swimming brief made of the same jazzy octopus print as the bikini. Matchy-matchy with the hubby. The pair will make a prodigious eyeful no matter where their yacht lays anchor.

Walking the path back to L'Anse à l'Âne I feel balanced,

hepped up by the fact I've settled into a foreign culture and plunged face to face into what I rightfully gauged to be a non-threatening situation. The encounter with Philippe Jean unfolded exactly as I anticipated—his flamboyance tempered by having been caught in the web of a murder investigation, his surrender when he realized that his ablility to control his future was under siege.

Granted, he didn't say much. But what he did say, what has now entered the investigative equation, could well prove crucial to confirming the identity of the brute who took a knife to Zach Russell.

He said something about someone who knew Zach. His brother, I think. Something about high school.

A few imprecise words. Nonetheless, fraught.

Spurring a shift of focus from Johnny to an unnamed brother. Seemingly a high school classmate of Zach.

To some that would be petty detail, a paltry scrap of information. But it finds me dialling Inspector Ailsa Bowmore while I sit with a BAM Pale Ale under a thatched umbrella at my preferred beach bar in L'Anse à l'Âne. Sad to say, Céline is not working today. The beer is a little less inviting, but still does the job.

A sudden, earnest voice in my ear. 'Sebastian, are you okay?'

A bit of a jolt from the speedy connection. 'I'm fine.'

'I was starting to worry.'

I'm touched. 'No need. Bare feet in the sand, a hand on a BAM.'

'Dare I ask?'

'A local beer.'

'I'm getting the picture.' Her tone has moderated. 'Besides the beer and the beach, all going as planned?'

Still, her concern has elevated my self-esteem. I smile into the phone.

'Indeed.' I take another drink of beer. 'I'm calling for a reason.'

'You've discovered something of interest, as far as the case is concerned?'

'To put it mildly.'

'What exactly?'

I detect a lack of surprise. In the eyes of Inspector Bowmore I have investigative cred. She's done with the small talk. Suddenly, she's all business.

I relate the encounter with Philippe Jean, play by strategic play. At the end repeating slowly the critical three sentences.

There's a pause. I wait for her response.

'So,' she says finally, 'where are you thinking you go from here?'

'A very good question,' trying not to sound presumptive, opening the gate for her, as lead RCMP officer, to confirm the urgency of investigating this elusive brother of Johnny Smith. Mounties thrive on taking charge.

'To be honest,' she says, 'I was expecting more.'

Sad. How disappointing that an officer of her stature should not know that what might on the surface seem trivial could, in fact, prove monumental.

'So you think it was worth the trip?'

My teeth grip my tongue.

I'm left with no choice but to readjust expectations.

'In fact, I do.' If I sound curt, so be it.

'You're thinking we need to track down and question Johnny Smith's brother?'

She could do better than state the obvious. 'If not the RCMP in Marystown, then I'll do it myself.' My exasperation no longer under wraps.

Silence. She's absorbing.

'I'll tell you what. I'll get in touch with Sergeant Windermere and put it out there.'

"Put it out there." Sounds like chitchat over coffee and donuts.

Is Bowmore not prepared to mandate Windermere to act? Is she content to fence-sit, thinking that insipid response is enough?

Silence. She's absorbing the fact that four thousand kilometres away I'm seething.

'I'll do what I can,' she says.

'Have a nice day.'

'Call me when you get back.'

Doubtful. 'Goodbye.'

We both end the call at the same time. That much we agree on.

Another BAM. And right away another call.

I picked up a text from Nick, sent five minutes ago. He wants to talk. I'm thinking the worst.

'Nick, what is it? Are you okay?'

'Hold on a minute.' Sounds like he's moving to someplace private.

'You don't sound like yourself,' he says.

'I got your text.'

'I'm okay. Getting there. You know.'

'Really?' I'm not convinced.

'You're in a sweat, Dad. What happened? You turned up something?'

'Maybe. Listen, Nick, I have a question. Think about this. Did you and Zach ever talk about his high school days? Was he bullied? You know, about being gay?' I give him a few seconds to get a fix on it.

'What the heck are you talking about?'

I speedily recount the showdown with Philippe Jean, anxious

to get to the point.'I figure there had to be something going on between Zach and this brother of Johnny Smith.'

'Could be,' Nick says finally.

'So he was bullied?'

'Maybe, I guess. I don't know. He didn't say.'

'Are you sure?'

'It's high school. You keep things to yourself. Maybe tell a friend you trust. You don't make a show of it.'

'I see.'

In fact, I've seen it for some time, just didn't admit it. He's not just talking about Zach.

'You come out when there's no hassle. When it's safe. You wait until university.'

'I get it.'

'Good.'

In the pause that follows is the echo of Nick's response.

'My turn now?' he says.

'What?'

'I asked you to call because I have news on the Emmeline front.'

For the moment I had forgotten. We backtrack.

'I just got off the phone to her.'

'Right.' Shift focus, regroup.

'Get this—that Newfoundland woman who's married and living on *route du Cap aux Basques,* she's from Lamaline. She's Johnny Smith's older sister.'

'You're kidding.'

'She moved here at least five years ago. Her husband's loaded. They got two kids. Her name is now Joy Monplaisir.'

'Like shit, really?'

'Yes, really. Emmeline is thrilled. She loves pronouncing Lamaline so that it rhymes with her own name.'

'Excellent.'

'You're thinking what I'm thinking.'

'That Johnny Smith (a) has quick and easy access to Saint-Pierre and (b) a sister who somehow became aware that Zach Russell was a student at the Francoforum.'

Nick is quick to add, 'And (c) has a brother-in-law who takes the cocaine Johnny's been smuggling and deals it in Saint-Pierre.'

A bit of a leap. But only a bit. 'That would make sense.' Nick is pumped, which makes two of us. Nevertheless, one step at a time. 'Let's stay focused on the sister. I want you to talk to Sasha privately and see if the sister's name rings a bell. If so, then maybe there's a link to her knowing Zach was at the Francoforum.'

'I won't see Sasha until tomorrow. In the meantime, should I tell Frederick?'

It jerks me to the fact that he and Samantha are in Saint-Pierre.

'I could go back to them and put you on speaker. We're in *Square Joffre*.'

I get the picture. The brawny RNC inspector on a park bench, a stone's throw from the headquarters of *la gendarmerie*, twiddling his meaty thumbs, primed to take a leap into the investigation.

'They picked up cappuccinos and *cannelés*. Mae recommended them.'

I see. Sharing tourist tidbits, were we? And what else I wonder? Their respective cynicism about *moi* jetting off to Martinique?

Take a breath, Sebastian. Chill. Get a grip.

You're backsliding into old resentments about your ex and her love life. Keep your head where it belongs—on what's going to boost the investigation. Frederick is not without his benefits to the case. The studmuffin is a very good cop.

And, so, a shot of intrigue to spice up the *pause café?*

I finally get to Nick's question. 'Sure.'

'It's Dad. He wants to talk to you guys.'

"Is willing" is more like it. Another breath. 'Hi, folks, how's it going? Enjoying Saint-Pierre?'

'We are,' says Samantha, rather restrained. She's unwilling to be effusive, I assume, for Nick's sake. Understandable. Also self-defeating.

'Very pleasant,' says Frederick. Two peas in a pod.

Moving right along. 'Okay, so . . . for the sake of time I'll let Nick fill you in on the details of what's transpired in Martinique. And what he's found out from talking with his *mère française*, Emmeline.'

'I'm good with that,' notes the inspector.

Not that I'm offering him a choice. 'Frederick, you need to contact your dog tracker friend. Have him connect you with Colonel Tremblay, then fill Tremblay in on the details.' (I thought of calling Tremblay myself, but as I said, Frederick has his benefits.) 'Just be aware that up to this point Tremblay hasn't put much stake in Philippe Jean. However, that's beside the point. Johnny Smith is the focus, so Tremblay will be all ears for what's been dug up about him.'

'I can handle that.' A slight edge of sarcasm, but extra points for compliance.

'In the meantime, I've alerted Bowmore at RCMP headquarters, and she and the detachment in Marystown are playing the ground game from that end.'

A pause radiating surprise. 'I see.'

"See" being the operative word. Let's keep it at "see," Frederick.

My exchange with Inspector Bowmore didn't exactly warrant the assertive tone, but knowing Frederick, he'd muscle himself into a bigger role than he needs to have. I'll do what it takes to drive home the fact that I'm in the lead, no matter that I'm not yet back home and into the thick of things.

I will be soon enough. 'I fly back tomorrow.'

'We catch the ferry in the morning,' says Samantha. 'We're both back to work on Tuesday.'

'In that case, Frederick, let's rendezvous as soon as we can after I get back.'

Rendez-vous—I like the savvy francophone lilt.

'I have a lot on, but I should be able to fit you in.' Once back on home turf, the cop needs control.

But two can play that game. 'Ditto. I'll check my schedule once I'm settled.'

'Do that. Shoot me a text.'

'*Pas de problème*,' with deliberate zing.

That's about it. No need for a fond goodbye.

Except to Nick. 'Talk to you soon. Your dad will be thinking about you.'

'Love ya.'

'You, too, pal.'

Despite the sun, the sand, and the BAM, I'm anxious to get home. I have one more call to make—to Mae—but that can wait. For now let's just walk the length of the beach a few more times so the Caribbean vibe is fully ingrained. There will come a time (mid-February) when I'll bemoan the fact that I don't have the option of escaping to such a nirvana. Let's strip to the minimum and let the sun do justice to this Newfoundland flesh too long blanched by clothes.

What few sunbathers are scattered along the beach pay no mind to me. They are too busy making sure the tanning rays are evenly distributed across their denuded physiques. And I thought I was going for minimal.

Holy *bazoomba*. I'm in France. These are continental young women. Topless is no big deal.

I avert my eyes like I was born yesterday.

Not for all that long. The years fly by, as does my *naïveté*. Such civilized tans, so nonchalant and, well, natural. There are times when I think I'm a repressed nudist.

Not that I gawk. A sweeping glance, a slower pace, an extra couple of treks along the full extent of the beach.

Just as the wantonness has run its course and I'm about to return to my discarded gear, one of the young women sits up. Out of the corner of my eye I see she's surveying the shoreline.

There's not much new to see except me. On impulse I look over to her, smile slightly, offhandedly, as if I'm some worldly Frenchman. My head rebounds, my mind implanted with the face observing me.

That of the young woman from the bar who normally delivers the BAM—Céline. Relaxing *au naturel* on her time off.

'*Pas de pluie aujourd'hui*,' she calls to me.

I stop and turn back. '*Pardon*?' Focusing on her words, as much as possible.

'*Pas de . . .* ?' I know *pas de*. And I know *aujourd'hui*.

'*Pluie*,' she says, extending both hands above her head and letting her fingers trickle down. How could I forget? The translation is, nonetheless, nothing short of tantalizing.

The body language does me in. Jeez.

Control, Sebastian. You rounded the corner into middle age a friggin' decade ago. Your hormones might still be up to scratch, but there's such a thing as age appropriateness.

Then again, look at the famous big boys for which age is no friggin' boundary. Look at Paul McCartney. *Let It Be*. Look at Clint Eastwood. *The Good, the Bad, and the Ugly*. Jeez.

And then there's Mae.

Gawd, why am I even allowing this to bang about in my head?

Move on, Sebastian. As tempting as it was, move on. Wave a sociable, judicious wave and gather your gear and take comfort in the fact she was even interested, considering what hunks her age populate the island's beaches.

'*À bientôt,*' she calls.

My French vocab also includes that phrase. But let's not go there.

I reward my self-control with a blowout meal at Pignon Nouvelle Vague. Entirely on my own dime, I will add.

I have no idea what the name means (something new, something vague?), but I've read a load of online reviews, including several declaring that of all the restaurants in Martinique specializing in seafood, it's at the top of the food chain.

A table for one with a panoramic view past the railing to the beach, the lights of Fort-de-France glinting in the distance. How pleasant, how restorative after a challenging day, as I set aside the passions (investigative and otherwise) and lose myself in a Kir Royale and the menu open before me. I breathe sumptuously and exhale slowly.

Kir Royale—a blending of champagne and crème de cassis, the priciest of their *apéritifs*. Royal recompense for my moral virtue.

And now for the priciest of the *entrées*. *Ravioles de fruits de mer, sauce crustacés.*

As I expected, seafood ravioli—wonderful. Together with the sauce—OMG, stunning, albeit not the least bit crusty, as I tell Lucien, the upbeat young waiter. The humour is lost on him, but Lucien smiles broadly at my *joie de vivre*. It's a boost to his own. We've hit it off. I suspect his English customers are generally more subdued.

A pour of *Château de Brégançon Cru Classé La Réserve*. '*Bon choix,*' says Lucien. '*Pour fruits de mer*—super cool.' He's eager to practise his English.

'The perfect pairing, as we would say.'

'*Pour la langouste grillée sauce créole—oui*, the perfect pairing.'

His pronunciation proved a challenge, but kudos for effort. 'Awesome, Lucien.'

From the list of *nos plats*, I'm shelling out top euro for what Lucien calls *notre spécialité*.

'Your signature dish.'

He has a go at that as well, again with questionable results. But, 'Awesome,' nonetheless.

From what I get from Lucien there are more *fruits de mer* coming my way. I don't ask him exactly which *fruits de mer*. I'm game for the surprise.

'*Voilà*, dude!' A chummy Lucien delivers a platter of clawless, spiny lobster-like shellfish, served on the half shell. The meat, cut into small chunks and something no doubt amazing done to it, lies along the length of the open shells. A dish of creole dipping sauce rests brilliantly nearby. I hardly want to mess with the arrangement.

Lucien motions with a hand in front of his chest. 'Thumbs up?'

I return the gesture. He smiles broadly. I encourage him to watch as I make my first foray into the shells.

It leads my taste buds into culinary bliss.

'Ah, bro, super cool.'

His stockpile of English slang needs refinement, but at this point I'm all about the meal. *La langouste grillée, le vin, l'ambiance—formidable*, as we say.

As is dessert. At Lucien's suggestion—*flan au coco maison*. Another signature dish.

Excellent. Crème caramel with the zing of coconut. To quote Lucien, when he returns to collect the empty plate, '*Un autre* thumbs up.'

He stiffens to the more formal version of himself, '*Maintenant, monsieur, un digéstif?*'

I love how the French ritualize alcohol consumption, extending it to the very end of a meal. A *digéstif* of course. Why not? I didn't come this far into the menu not to go for broke.

'Your signature *digéstif*, Lucien?'

He beams, then uses his thumb to suppress one finger while raising the other three. '*La trilogie de rhums vieux!*'

A trio of old rums? I was thinking Scotch, and I don't know much about aged rum. But then again, when in Rome.

My pre-trip googling led me to the fact that Martinique is famous for its *rhum agricole*. Most rum is distilled from molasses, but in Martinique it's distilled from sugarcane juice.

'*Trois Rivières triple millésime, Neisson rhum 12 ans, et La Favorite La Flibuste.*'

That bears repeating. '*Encore*, Lucien.'

It sings off his tongue once again. Whatever it is, it's music to my ears.

'Bring it on.'

In my customary whisky-tasting fashion—eye it, nose it, sip it, let it linger in the mouth, only then slowly swallow. Wicked.

Aged *rhum agricole*—who knew? Sweeter than whisky, but with a depth I never imagined. I take my time with all three. Imbibing, savouring, appreciating. Getting a buzz on.

There's been a considerable amount of imbibing over the last couple of hours. I'd say it's about time for '*L'addition, s'il vous plait.*'

When Lucien returns, I hardly give it a second look. First of all, I know that in France there's no need to figure out a tip— it's included in the bill—and second, the bill is in euros and who the heck cares how much it actually cost. Not me.

A swipe of the card in the machine and there it is—done. I wave off the offer of a receipt. Brian won't be laying eyes on it. And I don't need the reminder until it swamps my credit card statement.

'You know what they say, Lucien—*que será, será*.'

I might be flying a bit high, but I'm in the cockpit and in control.

'*Ça va, monsieur?*'

'*Ça va bien*, Lucien, my man.'

I hold out my hand. He extends his and I shake it robustly.

'Remember, Lucien, *que será, será*.'

And with that I weave my way past a couple of tables and out the door of the restaurant. And straight onto the beach. Well, wasn't that a friggin' great experience and a half.

I wonder if my favourite beach bar is still open? I wonder how you say nightcap in French?

It is open and *ooh la la*, my all-time favourite server has returned to work. *À bientôt* is right. She looks like she's been expecting me.

She's clothed this time, but my memory bank is in good working order.

Céline is very pleased to see me. I'm very pleased to see her.

Not looking quite so level-headed maybe, but you know, walking on sand can be a bit shifty at the best of times.

To land in a chair under one of those thatched umbrellas is for the moment my sole purpose in life, and that I accomplish *tout de suite*. Somewhat gracefully, I might add.

Céline is as approving as I am. 'BAM, *Sébastien?*'

That sounds so good, intimate even. But no, '*Pas de* BAM.' I have something else in mind. '*Rhum agricole, Céline, rhum agricole vieux*.'

'*Clément Rhum Vieux XO*?'

'Bring it on.'

'*Très cher, monsieur.*'

'*Très cher* or *pas de très cher*, bring it on. And make that a double.'

'*Une double dose?*'

'*Absolument.*' Money is there to buy experiences I always say. The double dose is a killer.

NINE

I STIR, SICK taste in my mouth, dull pain in my gut.

Half-open eyes detect dawn. There, where the sky meets the ocean. It looks that way. Hard to tell when you're flat out on the sand.

My aching head is angled to one side. Enough that I didn't choke on the vomit.

Small mercies. Someone must have angled it.

Jesus. I passed out at the beach bar and was left here. What's her name left me here. Thinking I would revive.

Revive like I'm trying to do now. Ignoring the fact that I feel like shit and could puke again at any moment.

All a miscalculation. All that money gone to waste.

I make it to a beach chair. I close my eyes to refocus.

I might feel like shit but I've felt worse and gotten over it. Acceptance is half the battle. Willpower the other half.

My phone. I pat my pockets. I have it. It tells me 5:32. It tells me I have a plane to catch just after noon.

Getting to the Airbnb has a sobering effect. It's daunting, that's true, but there are very few people around at this hour. I largely go unnoticed.

I collapse on the couch, with just enough brainpower to set

the alarm on my phone. I definitely need more sleep.

I get maybe three hours. The phone keeps ringing, to the point it wakes me enough that I pry my eyes open to see who's calling.

Mae. She's wondering why I haven't been in touch. Shit, I planned to, last night, after the meal.

The more times she hangs up, only to call again, the more it's obvious she's desperate to reach me. Maybe something has happened to Gaffer.

When she answers I hear Gaffer bark in the background. He sounds healthy enough.

'Just what the fuck is going on?' Her yell just about takes my ear off.

Whoa. If I wasn't wide awake before, I am now.

'What are you taking about?' It's what I can manage.

'That fucking picture.'

'Mae, what are you talking about?'

'Look at your messages.'

'What messages?'

'Look at your fucking messages.'

I do as I'm told.

Jesus.

Her hand covers her face, but it's Céline alright. I can tell by the naked breasts. And it's me all right, even though my eyes are closed. Even though my chest is also bare.

Good God.

Sent to both of us by one designer bastard—Philippe Jean. No caption.

'Good God, Mae. I was drunk. I passed out. It's a setup.'

'I fucking wasn't born yesterday.'

Or the day before, apparently. She needs to calm down. I need to calm down. One step at a time.

'Mae, believe me, it's a fake. The bastard set this up.'

There's silence, until finally, 'The boobs aren't fucking fake.'

'I'm sorry, I drank too much. I blacked out.'

Sorry is hardly going to do it.

'And then, and only then, did she tear off her top, haul open your shirt and plaster herself around you. Don't give me that shit.'

Not exactly "plaster" herself around me, but one of the boobs is in contact with my chest. 'It's not shit.' Rather weakly. I tried not to sound remorseful when there's no need to.

'Is that the best you can do?'

It's all I can do. But no, a picture is not worth a thousand words. It's bloody well not.

This is all going nowhere. This tirade over the phone is not accomplishing a damn thing. We need to talk face to face. Perhaps she'll have calmed down by then.

'I have a plane to catch. I get home tomorrow morning. We'll talk then.'

It's the best I can do.

Except, 'Mae, I'm sorry this happened.'

'So am I, fuck it.' She hangs up.

Needless to say, I've never heard her this angry. She has a right to be. And so have I, fuck it.

What the hell is that bastard Jean up to? Paying that floozie Céline to put the makes on me, then get that picture so he can run a fuckin' scam?

What the hell for? Payback for tracking him down? Making sure I don't talk to the cops about him because I'd have zero credibility once they get their eyes on that goddamn picture? So, what didn't he tell me? Did I let the bastard get away with murder?

He had my contact number, but how the hell did he get Mae's?

All questions that clog my hungover brain while I stuff my luggage and call a cab in my lousy French and wait the half-hour until the bloody driver finally shows up.

I need to calm down. The drive to the airport doesn't do it. The tedious line to get through security doesn't do it. The hopeless walk through duty-free thinking I could buy something to bring back to Mae doesn't do it. She'd likely fire it straight back in my face.

I sit in the lounge at the gate, suck on a bottle of water, and fume.

How the frig did he get Mae's number? Who had it to give to him? Racking my brain yields one, and only one, possibility. Monique, the mouthy owner of Impromptu in Saint-Pierre. Mae gave her a business card. I saw her take it. And for some reason she passed the contact number on to Philippe Jean. He knew Mae had been in the shop. He took a chance Monique might have her number. Came up with some excuse why he needed it. Or the two of them are in cahoots, for some fucking reason.

Who knows the details at this point? Who cares? He somehow got the number and royally screwed me.

The fuming continues once we're airborne. It only stops when I doze off, during which time I miss the meal. When I come to my senses, the trays have all been collected and everyone else is sitting back satiated, sipping on a last plastic cup of water before the plane lands.

A hungry, muted, 'Fuck.'

The word is muttered innumerable times between the flight landing in Montreal, the two-hour wait for the connection to Halifax, and another seven-hour wait overnight for the connection to St. John's.

PAL (misnomer) Airlines is set to arrive at 9:38 a.m. Seven minutes under the two-hour minimum for meal service. Water and cookies. Double fuck.

No, by shit, I'm not taking an overpriced cab from the stand at Arrivals. I text pal Ivo, my go-to taxi driver.

–You working? Pick-up airport. I'll be waiting outside.

Ivo doesn't let me down. He dekes in far enough away from Arrivals that he's unnoticed.

He flips open the trunk and deposits my bag inside. 'You look like shit.'

Ivo doesn't mince words. It's a Latvian trait.

'For good reason.' I refrain from going into details. Ivo doesn't expect them. Another Latvian trait.

We're out of the airport maze, me sucking on a Mentos, the only thing Ivo has on offer, when he unloads what's on *his* mind.

'In two weeks I fly home!'

'To Latvia?'

'Yessir.'

'What about Ash?' His Newfoundland girlfriend.

'We're getting married. She'll need permanent residence when we start our restaurant.'

Ivo came to Newfoundland to play professional hockey. He got injured. He hooked up with Ashley. Loves cooking, works two jobs—sous chef and taxi driver—to save enough money to go back home and start a restaurant. How we met is a long story, rife with ups and downs. Best left unrepeated.

'Good on ya, Ivo.' Returning home to open a restaurant has been his dream for as long as I have known him.

'You come visit, Mr. Synard. You'll love Latvia. You stay with me and Ash. We show you a good time.'

Not something that's likely to see the light of day. Latvia hasn't exactly been on any bucket list. Always sounded cold and severe.

'Liepāja, where we go—eight kilometres of beach on Baltic Sea. White sand, on and on. In summer—hot, hotter than Newfoundland.'

I'm afraid I've had it with sandy beaches.

'Latvian women—tall and very beautiful. You check the Net.'

Right.

Ivo adds roguishly, 'Or maybe you come and check our nudist beach.'

Right.

How about I chuckle and check out of the conversation until we're parked outside my house.

Ivo retrieves the case from the trunk and hands it to me.

'Latvia is part of the EU, right?'

'Yep.'

I open my wallet and dig through my pockets, unloading all my leftover euros. Not a lot, but Ivo resists, 'No, no, Mr. Synard. Too much.'

'I'm done with them. You'll have long connections. Buy yourselves a few meals.'

'We'll see you before we go, Mr. Synard. My treat.'

'Tim Hortons.'

'Deadly.'

The house is not empty. There's barking at the window even before I turn the key.

'Gaffer, what are you doing here?'

Not that I'm not excited to see him. I'm on my knees so he can have a concentrated bout of face-licking.

'Aren't you supposed to be still at Mae's? Didn't I say I would pick you up?'

He has no words to clarify the situation. I, however, suspect I know the answer. Mae has opted not to meet me. She dropped the dog off earlier this morning, before I was due to show up.

I see. She's still blatantly pissed.

All this to cope with when my focus should be the upsurge in the investigation, now that I'm back safe, and relatively sound.

Fine, if that's how she wants to play it, that's her choice. Petty, if you ask me.

I have other priorities. I sit at the kitchen table and mentally summarize where exactly I'll take the case from here. While scarfing down eggs, melted cheddar, and slabs of backbacon heaped between two halves of a defrosted and toasted English muffin. With a side of coffee brewed intensely black.

First on the agenda, follow-up with Bowmore—what's with Johnny Smith's brother? Second, with Nick—what's with Johnny Smith's sister in Saint-Pierre? Third, with Frederick—what's with the *gendarmerie* vis-à-vis the same sister, one Joy Monplaisir (née Smith)?

Which leaves follow-up directly with the colonel, now that I've got the goods on the bastard Philippe Jean. Even if I have to disclose the bare breasts scenario and risk blowing my credibility sky high?

I'm thinking that Tremblay, being French and all, will have a certain understanding of topless sunbathing and be able to see past its potential pitfalls for the innocent male. Laissez-faire and all that. An understanding of how a man might get caught up, through no fault of his own, in an intimate misadventure. A sensual faux pas.

I cannot *not* get in touch with Tremblay. He needs to come around to seeing that Phillippe Jean is a vital link to solving the case.

I refresh the coffee in the "Best Dad Ever" mug Nick gave me when he was eight, then sit in the comfy chair. I've decided to switch the follow-up list and call Nick first. Less potential for stress. He'll be just breaking for lunch.

'Hcy, Dad, you'rc back homc?'

'Jet-lagged but bright-eyed and energized. Gaffer at my side.'

'And everything went according to plan in Martinique?'

'One small hitch, not worth mentioning, but all good, back and ready to roll. Any luck with Sasha? Had she heard of Joy Monplaisir?'

'No, but I have big news about her husband.'

Really. 'Way to go.'

'Emmeline's sister-in-law has uncovered the name of Joy Monplaisir's husband's brother. In other words, Johnny Smith's brother-in-law's brother.'

Okay. I could ask him to repeat that, which would be pointless. 'So relatively speaking, who is it?' I'm no longer expecting much.

A trumpet blast. 'Théo!'

'Holy shit, you mean like the Théo of Amélie and Théo?'

'Exactly.'

'Emmeline—sleuth *extraordinaire*. Hug her for me.'

'She's getting off on it for sure. She's anxious to put out more feelers.'

'Sweet.'

Almost as sweet as the link between Johnny Smith and the hulk Théo. 'I'm thinking that if the brother-in-law is dealing cocaine, so is Théo,' I mutter to myself as much as to Nick.

'And Amélie was part of the action, at least to the point of protecting the boyfriend.'

'And to the point of disavowing any knowledge of Philippe Jean.'

'Exactly.'

Which reminds me, "There's something I need you to check out. Remember Impromptu, the shop where Zach first met Philippe Jean? Remember Mae and I were there and we got to know the owner? Her name is Monique. Check with Emmeline, see what she can find out about her.'

'Put out more feelers. She'll love it.'

'Tell her *bonne chance*.'

'Okay, I better go, I have an assignment due this afternoon. It needs a bit more work.'

That's good to hear. It means he's settled back into the program? I don't ask. Best to give him space, not say anything that might be mistaken for pressure.

'Love you, pal.' I take another drink of coffee.

'Love you, Dad. Say hi to Mae for me.'

I call Ailsa Bowmore without taking time to build myself up to it. That's a mistake.

'Hi Ailsa, it's Sebastian.'

'You're back. That's a relief.' A bit blunt there, inspector.

'True enough.'

'Everything went according to plan?'

'You could say that.'

'So, nothing new uncovered after we talked?'

'Not really.'

'You want to know if I followed up, about Johnny Smith's brother.'

That would be it. She pauses, as if it had been a question.

My silence tells her I didn't take it as one. An inaudible prod for her to continue.

'So, I contacted Staff Sergeant Windermere in Marystown.'

Again a pause. I fail to see the need. Placidly I dig in my heels.

'And she investigated,' she notes.

God, it's like pulling teeth.

'You were right. Johnny Smith does have a brother.'

As if it were ever a point of debate. Enough. 'Did she track him down? What did he say? Was she able to confirm if the brother and Zach Russell were in high school together?'

'In fact, Jody Smith and Zach Russell did graduate together from high school two years ago. Following which they both enrolled at MUN.'

Finally, we're getting somewhere.

Jody, Johnny, and Joy. I've heard of parents naming all their kids using the same letter of the alphabet. But not for the first two letters of the name, plus the last. A screwy synchronicity if you ask me.

'And Jody is still at MUN I take it?'

'That we haven't confirmed at this point.'

'You mean you haven't checked it out.' There's an undercurrent of *why the frig not?* It's a pretty simple undertaking for someone with cop credentials.

'This is not the only file needing our attention. As you will appreciate.'

Not that it would burn up a lot of friggin' time and resources. In other words it's not a priority. In other words Bowmore has no faith that it would lead anywhere useful. Like to a face-to-face with Jody Smith, armed with a barrage of questions to determine what exactly his relationship is with his brother, and his mother. And just what the hell was it with Zach Russell.

I'm pissed. Pissed, knowing I can't let on to the inspector that I'm pissed.

'When you find out, let me know.' Best if I pull the plug before my restraint disintegrates.

'Will do.'

Will friggin' do. 'Talk to you later.' Jab end call. Grit teeth.

I need breathing space.

I leave the house with Gaffer and head across the street and along to the public grounds surrounding Government House, our regular dog-walking destination.

While Gaffer sniffs about any which way, I focus—deep breath through the nose, fill the belly, hold for four seconds, exhale through the mouth for as long as possible. Allow the stress to wash away. Repeat.

We pass but a few other walkers on our route. I nod each time, without missing the internal rhythm—long inhale, hold, longer exhale. A rhythm I also manage while bending down, bag in hand, to retrieve the prerequisite poop. I'm starting to feel like myself again.

So much so, that after depositing the bag in a trash can, I leisurely take to one of the park benches, then switch breathing exercises to one with the added benefit of empowerment.

I read about it online. It's called "lion's breath." I've not attempted it before, but if there was ever a time to give it a go, this is it.

Long breath in through the nose, hold it for the count, exhale through the mouth, thrust out the tongue, gaze slightly upward, emit a pronounced 'Haaa . . .'

I like it. I like the energy. I like the release. I like how it clears the throat, relaxes the neck and facial muscles.

Gaffer is not so sure. He looks at me, confused, emitting a sharp bark. I rub his head and repeat.

'Haaa . . .' Empowerment? Absolutely. It's not called "lion's breath" for nothing.

Gaffer repeats his bark. He'll get used to it.

'Haaa . . .'

'Is something wrong?'

I hadn't noticed the elderly woman with the walking stick coming up behind me.

I try not to look embarrassed. 'Yoga,' I tell her. Which is true. It's often part of a yoga workout. Also something I read online.

'No mat? I always thought yoga folks had a mat.'

'I go matless . . . generally . . . especially here, you know, the Lieutenant-Governor could be looking out the window.'

'I see. I hadn't thought of that.' She bends down slowly and pats Gaffer. 'Very good. Continue.' And ambles away.

A sweetheart. The older the fiddle the sweeter the tune, as the saying goes.

Gaffer agrees. He watches her as she turns along a path toward a surprising cluster of blue hydrangeas.

It seems to strike him as a good note on which to head for home. He leads the way, tenderhearted mutt that he is, as I emit one last 'Haaa . . .'

I'm in a constructive headspace. I've been working against the odds, but as I drive toward RNC headquarters and my meeting with Frederick Olsen, I'm categorically upbeat.

A terse exchange of texts has set the meeting for mid-afternoon. As I enter his office I see the inspector is looking equally positive. It could be a front, but maybe not. Maybe I misjudged him during that last phone call. With any luck, we might just find ourselves on the same wavelength.

'You're looking good, Sebastian. A bit of a tan. Still feeling that tropical energy. A change is as good as a rest and all that.'

Putting down some small talk before getting to the nitty-gritty. Nice. 'And while I was at it, I discovered some excellent aged rum.'

We share smiles. Bodes well. A brief pause. Looks like he's waiting for me to take the plunge.

'Tracking down Philippe Jean was well worth it. The bit about the younger brother is significant. We're now dealing with the three J's, as I call them—Johnny Smith; Joy, the older sister, in Saint-Pierre; and Jody, that younger brother, high school classmate of Zach Russell, and perhaps still a student at MUN. Bearing in mind that Zach was their second cousin.'

Frederick takes a moment, perhaps to reconfigure his assessment of the trip. 'So what's your take on the brother?'

'Not yet in a position to know exactly. That will take confronting him.'

'So you know his location?'

I might as well hit him with it. 'I was hoping you might make a couple of calls. I don't know for sure if he's still at university. Or, if he is, then if, by chance, he's in one of the student residences.'

'I see. Shouldn't be a problem.'

So quick it rattles my timing. I smile ineptly. 'That's good of you.'

I could have been more effusive, but, make no mistake, I need to keep our relationship balanced. No way can I have him think he has the upper hand.

'I relayed the information about Joy Monplaisir to Colonel Tremblay, as you asked. I'm afraid he already knew.'

I refuse to look surprised, or disappointed. 'Good. Their investigation is moving along.'

'As you would expect.'

Frederick is playing hardball. 'But did he know anything about a younger brother?'

'I assume Staff Sergeant Windermere and Inspector Bowmore have updated him.'

Strike two. Olsen has been in a huddle with Bowmore.

No way, Frederick, am I about to strike out. Which means I need to make a move on Jody Smith ASAP, before Bowmore gets in ahead of me.

'I need you to make the calls. Sooner rather than later.'

He's not fond of plainclothes pressure. It takes a moment, but he nods. 'Would you mind stepping outside for a few minutes?'

I do without hesitation, or expectation. I take a seat in the public waiting area, phone in hand, time-checking repeatedly.

Nine minutes later Frederick pops back and gestures to me to rejoin him in his office.

'Yes, to your first question. He's enrolled at MUN for the fall semester. And as for the second, he's on the list for Shiwak Hall.' Adding, with the scent of sarcasm, 'Would you like to know the room number?'

Very nice all the same. 'Thank you.' He retrieves a pad of sticky notes and a pen.

It strikes me that the MUN student residences have tighter security than when I lived in one decades ago. I wouldn't be able to just show up and knock on the fellow's door. I press my luck. 'By chance would his application happen to include a phone number?'

Olsen looks up at me. I shrug. He takes his time, to make it clear his command of the situation is still intact. He returns to the pad of sticky notes, scratches on it a second time and hands the note to me.

'Thanks.'

'All I ask is you don't make me sorry I did this.'

'I won't.' I get up to leave.

'And, Sebastian. Watch your ass.'

'That too.' As I approach the door I turn back. 'If I need backup, I'll be in touch.'

I'm out the door before he has chance to respond.

I'm home in the comfy chair, Gaffer asleep at my feet, and into a dram of *Eddu Brocéliande* when I punch into my phone the final number on the sticky note. It's early evening. A weeknight. Past suppertime. Assignments due, maybe.

My heart is racing. Probably because I haven't convinced myself I know how to deal with this, if and when he answers.

'I think you have the wrong number.'

He's not seeing any caller ID. I've disengaged it.

'Would this be Jody Smith?'

A slight pause, but then, 'Yes.'

'I'm looking into the death of Zach Russell. I'm not a cop . . .'

The line's suddenly dead.

The kickback was not a surprise. He thinks he's rid of me.

I think not. Time for a quick change to the second option.

Ending the call the way he did was instant confirmation that he's got something to hide. He's scared.

To my mind so scared that he'll answer the text that I'm about to send.

I compose it offline, reworking it until what he reads will give him, intelligent fellow I presume him to be, firm reason to get back to me before uniformed police officers come pounding at his door.

–The cops have a fix on you. I understand how they operate. I can tell you how to deal with them when they show up. Get back to me. Sebastian Synard. Private detective.

Straightforward, only as long as it needs to be. Enough to trigger a response. If not right away, not long after.

Exactly. My phone delivers its no-nonsense text tone.

–Back steps of dining hall in half hour

I detect desperation. Perfect.

He likely expects me to get back to him for more details. No need. I know exactly the dining hall he means. The same dining hall and the same steps as when I lived on campus. The same half-dozen steps patronized for a late-night toke.

In twenty minutes I'm sitting on one of them, beneath the tall white wooden columns of the portico that defines the rear of the Gushue Dining Hall. I'm the only one around, except for a few students strolling between the several student residences that circle the open space in front of me. For the most part it's grass-covered and scattered with leaves that have fallen from the dense, towering maples. We're into fall, and I feel the chill from the concrete.

I'm not waiting long. It can only be him, approaching reluctantly along a side path. He's wearing jeans and a black MUN hoodie.

'Sebastian,' I volunteer quietly. 'You must be Jody.'

He stares at me from the base of the steps, unwilling to come any closer or say anything. The situation is untenable.

'Follow me.' I walk down the few steps and past him, onto the grass and toward a cluster of empty, square-shaped picnic tables.. In the semi-darkness I choose one and take to one of its four side benches. He wanders cautiously near and eventually seats himself opposite me. We stare at each other across the three-foot width of the tabletop. My hands, locked together, rest in front of me. He sits stiffly, arms folded.

At least he's there, at least he hasn't changed his mind and copped out.

Yet there's no point in going soft on him. 'You want to know what's behind all this. Pay attention and when I'm finished you decide if you have anything to say. We got all night. The cops are not likely to show up before morning.'

He continues to stare at me, straight-faced, rigid.

'I'm one of the three people who discovered the body of Zach Russell, off the beach in Saint-Pierre. It so happens I'm a private detective. The investigation has led to you being what could be called "a person of interest," stemming from the fact that you're the brother of Johnny Smith, who is thought to have had contact with Zach prior to his death.'

'What the fuck? You think Johnny did it.'

He's come alive, and in the process jumped multiple steps

ahead. There was a helluva lot going on in his head. Which is staying there, for now.

'And what the fuck else are you saying—that I had something to do with it?'

'You're not listening. It's an investigation. The cops are not about to show up with an arrest warrant.'

One hand is rubbing against his forehead. He looks down, at nothing.

'Let's set a few things straight. What was your relationship with Zach Russell?'

He looks up at me. 'Why the hell should I tell you anything?'

'Because if you are involved, you're fucked.' That jerked him to his senses. 'And if not, then I can give you good advice.'

I have his unconditional attention.

'I wouldn't want him hurt. It wasn't me.'

'Like I said, what was your relationship with Zach Russell?'

'He broke it off. I was over it.'

I see. So, more than former classmates. More than university friends. More than second cousins.

'How long had you two been together?'

'Together? Since we started at MUN. We were roommates.'

'And before that?'

'Nobody knew anything.'

'But they suspected?'

He looks away. 'We never got along anyway.'

'You mean Johnny?'

'With Johnny it wasn't only that. It was a lot of other shit.'

'Like what?'

'Dope. He was big into it. I wasn't. He had dropped out of school. I didn't. He and Mom . . . I couldn't wait to get outta there. They blamed it on Zach. Said he screwed me up.'

'Your mother was on your case?' I can see Johnny, and maybe . . . . But she was his mother after all.

'It was worse after Austin took off.'

I wait for more.

'They weren't married. But he kept it livable.'

A longer wait.

'I didn't fit in. That's fucking all it is. I'm out of it, now. When I go back I don't stay. I've made my own life.'

Easier said than done I would think. Made worse by the breakup with Zach.

'Who's this guy Nick?' he snaps. 'You questioned him?'

It knocks me for a loop.

Who told him his name? I doubt it was Zach. Johnny maybe. Or the sister.

He's staring, insisting on an answer.

'He wasn't near there at the time it happened. He can prove it.'

To tell him anything more would only screw up any progress I've made.

'So can I. I can prove I was nowhere near Saint-Pierre.'

I'm sure he can. That, of course, is not the point. 'But Johnny was. And so was Joy.'

His circumspection deflects to anger. 'Now the fuck you're bringing my sister into it. She had nothing to do with anything.'

'But Johnny could have? That's right, isn't it? You don't trust Johnny. He's impulsive. He hated Zach.'

The fellow draws back. He jams a fist against his mouth, forcing control of his reaction.

His breathing is erratic. When he releases his fist, he struggles to get out the words. A few emerge. 'Not enough to do that to Zach.'

That being murder. That being still an open question.

I hold back. I move to a side bench closer to him.

'Listen to me. The cops are going to expect answers to their questions. Don't lie to protect your brother. It will only make it worse for you. If it's any reassurance, I believe you, I don't think you had anything to do with Zach's death. You're involved because there's the possibility that someone in your immediate family did. You can't change that. You can only deal with it. You said yourself you're making your own life. We both know all this has made it a helluva lot harder. But fight it, get a hold on yourself. You deserve to get through this.'

He takes moment before he gets to his feet. I walk with him back toward Shiwak Hall. He doesn't stop me.

It's not far, but the few minutes bring no more than troubling silence. Until we're standing together outside the main entrance.

'You have my number. I'm here if you need me, Jody. If it gets to the point you think you want a lawyer, I can help.'

Nothing breaks through his reticence. He turns and heads inside.

I walk back to where I've parked my car. It's colder now. Before long winter will close in on us.

TEN

OF COURSE, ALL this time Mae is in my thoughts. I try to hold them at a distance, when I can manage it.

Which, frankly, is not often.

Time heals. Or so it's said. I'm not sure I'm willing to take the chance.

It's reached the point—all of twenty-four hours after arriving home—of steeling myself to forge ahead and try to resolve the situation.

Maybe forge is the wrong word. I pick up my phone to call, but in the end decide to text. It's less dicey.

–Hi. How goes it? You'll be happy to know Gaffer has settled in nicely.

From my perspective, pretty conciliatory.

–How about you? Settled in? Nicely?

Not sure how to take that.

–Yes. A lot happening with the investigation and all.

–No doubt. You'll have to fill me in. When you get around to it.

Hard to judge the tone behind those last few words. I press ahead, optimistically.

–Absolutely. Anytime.

–Cut the shit, Sebastian. We need to talk. I'll be home from work by 6.

Okay. Deep breath. Point taken. I need a response.

–Okay

(Without a period after it. I included one, then cut it. I thought it looked less aggressive. Now, I'm thinking it looks wimpy. Jesus, even texting puts me in a sweat.)

Six o'clock is eight hours away. I walk Gaffer. Eat breakfast. Get my mind and butt in gear. Enough of this crap.

I fire off a text to Inspector Bowmore. I need a face-to-face ASAP.

–Okay. 11 in my office.

I show up ten minutes early and wait. The receptionist alerts the inspector. She'll see me right away.

'You're stressed, Sebastian.'

I skip a response. Instead I spew out all I got from Jody. Right down to my belief that he wasn't directly involved, that likely it was Johnny acting on his own, getting back at Zach because Johnny figured Zach screwed up his brother.

'This is all very interesting,' she says.

'Interesting is an understatement.'

She's skeptical. No surprise. She's not about to admit that a PI might be one step ahead.

She smiles. I wouldn't say patronizing, but close to it.

Regardless, I get a grip. 'So, what's your game plan?' Assuming she has one.

'I'll contact Staff Sergeant Windermere.'

'Of course.'

'We'll take it from here.'

Really? I do the groundwork and the RCMP step up and help themselves to the payoff? I think not.

'Keep me in the loop. I'll be standing by.' To put it as tolerantly as I can.

'I'm not sure that will be necessary, Sebastian. As you would know, confronting a suspect is unpredictable. It's best you keep your distance. Besides which, you don't want to be going all the way to Lamaline or to Saint-Pierre, wherever Johnny Smith might be at the moment, just on spec.'

Just on spec. The inspector pauses, thinking I need time to come to terms with it. How decent of her.

Then she adds, 'And that's not to say we don't appreciate all you've done. We do. Absolutely.'

Please, let me vomit here and now.

It's best if I withdraw before I lose it altogether and spew out what's roaring around in my mind. Then regret it afterwards.

'I see.' I stand up. 'In that case when will I hear from you?'

'That depends.'

'On what you find?'

'Or if, indeed, we find anything.'

I crack a smile, turn, and leave, faking a bloody look of satisfaction past the receptionist and out of the building.

I recover in time. The lion's breath is something of a help.

Calling Zach's parents does more than touch base with the trusting couple who hired me. It's the opportunity to relate in detail what their financial faith has accomplished in the short few days since I left their house in Lamaline.

They have me on speaker phone. I spare nothing. It builds to a rigorous conclusion.

Brian declares, 'So you think that Johnny the young fucker is the one who done it?'

'You could say that. But, Brian, don't go anywhere near him. Don't get involved. Let the cops handle it.'

'So, the police know everything you've told us?' asks Lisa.

'They do.'

'They must be very thankful to you for going to Martinique.'

One would think. 'And thankful to you two for backing me to go.' If I were them, I wouldn't hold my breath for any vote of thanks.

Before ending the call I promise to keep them updated, although, in this case, I like to think the RCMP will get in ahead of me. At the least, Lisa and Brian deserve some semblence of a resolution.

And now, what's next on the daily planner? Hang out on the sidelines and let it all unfold wherever and however the cops lay their hands on Johnny Smith, the (quote/unquote) young fucker.

I'm tempted to call Colonel Tremblay for the view from ground zero, but I'm not sure what that would accomplish. No doubt he and Windermere have had their rap session. I can only imagine what they would have said about me.

Gaffer is as enthusiastic about his kibble as I am about the granola bar that I unearthed from the pantry. I suffer through it in the hopes that it will boost my energy level and prompt me into cooking up something substantial.

On the other hand, Gaffer takes the bits of the bar that I slip him as an exciting alternative to kibble. 'One fella's meat is another fella's poison.' He agrees, hoping for more.

Just as he finishes the bar a text message inserts itself into the state of play.

Jody Smith. I'm taken by surprise, but pleased.

–I need to see you. We need to talk some more.

This is promising. Right away I'm thinking this is about to put me back in the lead, one step ahead of the cops.

–No problem. Where? When?

–Same place. Same time.

Which, as I remember it, was roughly eight o'clock. I was thinking sooner. I was thinking urgent. But I can live with whatever he wants. He needs the anonymity of darkness.

–See you then.

Nothing back. But all good. There's something weighing on him and he's trusting I'm the one to tell. Something decisive. I feel it.

One slight issue. Mae is expecting me sometime after six. It's not going to work to deal with that turmoil prior to seeing Jody. I will just have to let her know it'll likely be later rather than sooner by the time I get to her place.

I do just that.

–See you around nine.

I think of adding "due to a situation beyond my control," but think better of it. I type "Looking forward to it." I scrap that too. No, it's a minefield. Keep it simple. Hope for the best. In any case, there's no reply.

Conjuring up the scenario with Mae leaves me in a bit of a sweat. I don't usually resort to a mid-afternoon dram, but what the heck.

Besides, I have the *Eddu Brocéliande* to work through for *Distill My Reading Heart*, the blog that I'm not paying sufficient attention to, due to situations beyond my control.

The blog is still in need of a book. Something French to complement the *Eddu*. I have my eyes on a murder mystery set in Saint-Pierre and Miquelon, given there is indeed such a beast. I picked up a copy while we were there—*Dans les brumes de Capelans* by Olivier Norek.

The author is, no surprise, French. He's published, by last count, ninc novcls, four of which have been translated into English.

But not the one I'm holding in my hand.

Have you ever tried reading a book using the translation app on your iPhone, one page at a time?

It's tedious, to put it mildly. But it does fill up an afternoon, just getting through the first ten chapters. The *Eddu*, I will note, eases the tedium and heightens the intrigue. However, with close to forty chapters yet to go, I'm uncertain if the whisky will hold out to the end. I'm trusting that by then, firmly in the story's grip, I won't care.

In the meantime, I recork the bottle, put together an alcohol-absorbing meat-and-potatoes meal and, to be on the safe side, make the decision to walk instead of drive to the encounter with Jody.

The trek in the dark takes a half-hour, making allowance for the drizzle. My jacket is waterproof and my timing spot-on.

There's shelter to be found under the portico at the top of the steps where I sat waiting for that first encounter with him. It's brightly lit and through the bank of the tall windows of the dining hall I can see students finishing up their meals. I lean against one of its pillars and check my phone for messages.

He appears suddenly, out of the darkness to the right of me, dressed the same except his hood is up, shielding him from the drizzle.

He stops, startled by the light, and seemingly having to shield his eyes from it.

He's sure it's me . . . but there's something . . .

He bolts in my direction just as I'm slipping my phone in a pocket.

What the fuck . . .

He slams me to the ground. My head scrapes the concrete.

He jerks me sideways, flat on my back, planting himself on my gut, my arms locked under his shins.

I'm too fucked up to know what the hell he's about. Except for what little registers through the brain fog—the face framed by the hoodie. Enough of the face to see it's something like him but not him.

The brain fights to make sense of it.

His goddamn brother.

Who leans into my face, growling, 'I could fuckin' knife you. You got that? I could but I won't, like I didn't do it to Zach Russell. You fuckin' got that?'

He looks up. I can't see what he sees, but it must be someone staring through a dining hall window.

'You fag,' he yells into my face, 'you fuckin' fag.'

He scrambles off me and tears away.

He's gone. I'm stunned. Submerged in disbelief, struggling to the surface.

Around me converges a herd of students, some still chewing.

One kneels in front of me, shouting 'You all right?'

I might be stunned but I'm not deaf. 'I'm okay.'

He scans the others. 'Who thinks we should call 911?'

There's a flurry of hands digging out cellphones.

'No.' I mutter. 'I'm okay. I just need a second.'

'Check for a concussion.'

'No,' I mutter, louder. 'Just give me a second.'

A girl is suddenly on her knees on the other side of me. 'I'm in third-year Nursing. Let's try sitting him up.'

'I can do it myself.'

Well almost. Her hand now moves from supporting my back to exploring my head.

'Sizable hematoma,' she pronounces. She moves the same hand in front of my eyes. 'How many fingers?'

'Two . . . I think.'

'Double vision. Do you feel a need to vomit?'

'Not particularly.'

'Not yet at least. Any tingling in your arms? Restlessness in your legs?'

'Jesus,' I mutter.

'I say we call an ambulance.'

'Absolutely,' confirms her accomplice.

The 911 operator is inundated.

The Health Sciences Centre is a stone's throw from the university. I'm wheeled into Emergency, a waste of taxpayers' money. Apropos of which, I'm sent home within an hour.

A mild concussion. The two fingers merged into one. I verify the day of the week and the sum of 30 plus 22. I walk a very straight line. After which the doctor signs off on me and turns his attention to something more life-threatening.

In the taxi, I still feel no urge to vomit. In the comfy chair no tingling of arms or restlessness of legs. The overly zealous Nursing student would be relieved.

Gaffer takes it all in stride. It's not his first time coming to grips with the aftermath of a bash to my head.

And if there's an upside to a "mild" concussion, it's that there's absolutely no need to alert family and/or significant other.

Fuck. I forgot about seeing Mae.

Understandable from my perspective, given the mayhem, but from hers . . . I'd say she's blown a gasket.

I'm on the phone to her. 'You're not going to believe this . . .'

'Try me.'

'I would have showed up . . .'

'But for what, Sebastian? I have no time for excuses. This is serious. In case you haven't figured it out, our relationship depends on it. I've had enough. And forget texting. I'm going to bed.'

As if my sanity hasn't already been tested.

Just what the hell does she want from me?

Whether the urge is medically sound or not, what I want is whisky. The more independent-minded the better. Which would be maverick Laphroaig, iconic for its peaty, seaweedy, *medicinal* traits. Bring the bugger on.

I'm in a sure-as-hell homeopathic funk when the doorbell rings. Gaffer leaps from his section of the comfy chair and races to the door, barking madly.

Could it possibly be Mae, having had second thoughts?

It's Frederick.

'You must have missed my text.'

That would be the case. 'Come in. You're just in time. I know Laphroaig is not your thing . . .'

'You okay? How's the head?'

My quizzical look begs the question.

'Word gets around. MUN Security. They're required to inform us of any incidents.'

'I get a smack to the head and the whole world knows.'

By this time we're sitting down and I'm holding up the bottle and an empty Glencairn glass.

'I'll make an exception. Keep it small.'

A paltry pour of Laphroaig is a challenge. I do my best.

He takes a sip. 'You'll be happy to know the perpetrator has been arrested.'

My glass falls from my lips. 'Johnny Smith is in custody?'

'He was caught on security cameras pouncing on you and then having a go at his brother outside Shiwak Hall. They exchanged the hoodies they were wearing, but before long it turned into a yelling match. Johnny lunged for him, but Jody broke free and escaped inside. Johnny was left standing there.

Not for long, but long enough that a MUN patrol car showed up just as he ran off. They called in the RNC.'

Frederick stops for another sip of whisky. Reinforcement, I'm thinking, for his decision to divulge the specifics of police procedure, presumably without informing the higher-ups.

'To make a long story short, together they blocked the exit to the parking lot where he left his truck, then cornered him in the maze of walkways between the Library and the Arts Building. He didn't know whether he was coming or going. The security guys at MUN might not be cops but they know their campus.'

'So where's the shithead now?'

'In the lock-up, charged with assault. For now. The RCMP have bigger things in mind. We're meeting first thing in the morning.'

'I should be there.'

'That's not for me to decide,' he says, caution in his voice.

I'm more or less pissed, but, when I think about it, not surprised. The chain of command must get prickly when the RNC teams up with the Mounties.

'Inspector Bowmore has got your number. Correct?'

'I assume you mean phone.' Humour helps. 'Correct.'

'Let's wait and see how it plays out.'

Not as if I have a choice. 'Yes, let's do that.'

I don't push it. And, of course, I can't show anything but gratitude for him showing up and giving me the scoop.

I hold up the Laphroaig, needlessly. 'A top-up?'

It's the incentive he needs to make his getaway. He gives Gaffer a quick pat and makes for the door.

'Thanks, Frederick. I know this wasn't in your job description.'

'No problem. As long as you're no worse for the wear.'

'Right on.'

It's about as chummy as we ever get.

Gaffer and I share a restless night. He's being empathetic.

I'm being dysfunctional. I hate floundering, not knowing what to do next.

No, I won't attempt to get back in touch with Mae. It is not the way I want to start my day. Let her stew in her resentment. If that's what's she's doing.

And no, I won't call Bowmore and plead my case. Let her make the first move. If she wants me at the meeting, she wants me at the meeting.

I need positivity.

I'm about to pour my third cup of coffee when it shows up.

'Hey, Dad.'

He's sounding reasonably upbeat. This I like. This does me good.

'Great to hear your voice. I'm missing you. How's it going?'

'Missing you too. It's going okay. Getting up to the half-way mark, so, you know, that's good.'

'Absolutely.'

I stop at that.

'And Emmeline, she's fine?'

'That's why I'm calling. She's got something new to report.'

'Lay it on me.'

'She's not sure it means anything but Monique, who you asked about, has been to Martinique. Several times. She closes her shop every February and goes to Guadeloupe or Martinique for the month.'

'How did Emmeline find out that?'

'It's Saint-Pierre. Small town, no secrets. And, you know, she has her ways.'

'So . . . we're thinking Monique could have known Philippe Jean before he showed up in Saint-Pierre.'

'Or even encouraged him to come,' Nick says.

'For whatever reason. Maybe not just to market swim trunks.'

'Maybe never to market swim trunks. Maybe that was just a front.'

A web of possibilities. Plenty to send Lieutenant Clément Charpentier sniffing in Monique's direction.

'Emmeline figures she'll go to the shop and drop a few comments about Martinique to see how Monique reacts.'

I think not. 'That's best left to the *gendarmes*. They'll be pissed if it's not. Plus, Emmeline I figure is not someone who shops at Impromptu. Monique might think something is up.'

'Emmeline will be disappointed.'

'Tell her not to worry. Her sleuthing has already paid big dividends.'

'I'm not sure I can figure out how to say that in French.' He chuckles.

Chuckling is very good. Wonderful, in fact. I can't say anything but I'm thinking maybe Nick has rounded a corner.

A good point at which to switch focus. I'll keep it simple, avoid the details.

'This is under wraps. Just between me and you, okay.'

'No worries.'

'The cops arrested Johnny Smith.'

'You're kidding.'

The Reader's Digest version is not enough to satisfy him. But we've run out of time. He's got to get back to class.

'Call me tonight. I want it all. Don't hold back. I can handle it.'

On that note, 'Talk to you soon.'

'See ya, Dad.'

'Hang in there. Before you know it, the term will be over and you'll be home.'

There I go again. Self-control out the window.

'Once the father, always the father.'

The father of a profoundly lovable kid. I hang up and take a deep breath to sabotage the tears.

Just when you think your alliance with the police (RCMP, RNC, *et* GN-SPM) is beyond repair and you should stick to tour guiding, the iPhone rings. It's Inspector Ailsa Bowmore.

'Sebastian, we need you. Are you free to come to my office?'

Free as a fucking bird. 'Sure.'

'The sooner the better.'

Put out the welcome mat.

In twenty minutes I'm standing directly on it.

A light, but confident knock. Inspector Bowmore answers the door in next to no time. Remarkable.

'Come in, Sebastian. We're very pleased you could join us.' Equally remarkable.

Us being Inspector Olsen, as expected.

As half-expected, Staff Sergeant Windermere.

As totally unexpected, Colonel Tremblay and Lieutenant Charpentier.

I circle the room with a sequence of nods, ending with a substantive 'Good morning.'

They reciprocate in turn. 'Good day. Good day. *Bonjour. Bonjour.*' Firmly but not without generosity of spirit.

The room is teeming with their self-assurance. Nevertheless, I'm not claustrophobic, per se.

'Let me start by noting, Sebastian, that you're among friends.'

Which to my mind acknowledges the fact that before I arrived it was a matter of some debate. However, we won't go there.

'Thank you. *Merci.* I'm here, I presume, to be of help to you, in whatever way I can.'

'Shall we move along then,' Inspector Bowmore says, firmly in her role as convener. 'Let me begin by informing you that the report of the autopsy has been received.' She turns to Colonel Tremblay, who motions to her to continue. 'Zach Russell died of drowning, accelerated by the sudden loss of blood due to the severing of his right femoral artery. A lesion to the back of the head was a further contributing factor, but the head trauma was not deemed sufficient in itself to have caused his death.'

'I see.' I hear the words echoing through a courtroom, demanding retribution.

The inspector pauses briefly. 'Shall we move on?'

'Certainly.' A quick change of direction. I find a grip.

'As we are aware, Sebastian, you took it upon yourself to travel to Martinique. And there you tracked down a certain Philippe Jean, correct?'

'Correct.' Which is old news to everyone present.

'Do you believe, therefore, that Philippe Jean played a direct role in the death of Zach Russell?'

Okay, put me to the test straight away.

'That has yet to be determined.'

'You mean it needs further investigating.'

'When I first questioned Philippe Jean I thought possibly not, that it may just have been bad luck on his part that he was on the beach prior to the attack. And if Johnny Smith were there, hiding out, maybe Philippe Jean wasn't aware of him. Now I'm not so sure.'

'What made you change your mind?'

A pause, a doubly useful one—allowing me to consider exactly what I should say, and Tremblay to translate the finer points of what I've already said to the lieutenant.

'Philippe Jean, as I discovered and as you know, met Johnny Smith at a bar in Saint-Pierre and the two later snorted cocaine together. Now I'm wondering was there more to it than that. Had they known each other all along? Could Johnny be back into action with cocaine that's come from South America via Martinique and that Philippe Jean is involved in getting it to him? Maybe this time Johnny is smuggling it from Saint-Pierre to Newfoundland, not the other way around.'

I look about the room. I can't read their expressions. Skepticism or repressed admiration?

'In that case was there anything that Philippe Jean said or did while you were in Martinique that led you to this conclusion?'

I've been in a sweat about this very question since I entered the room. In a sweat that it would come down to the business of the photograph. Opening myself to ridicule, and no telling what else. If Frederick were to tell Samantha, she would have a friggin' field day. On top of which I would have to convince everyone in the room it was a set-up. No way can I come out of that looking like anything but a womanizing little shit.

'Not really. I just had this feeling, you know.'

They don't know.

'Nothing tangible?' asks Frederick. 'Nothing hard and fast?'

Seriously, Frederick?

'Not really. A gut feeling more than anything.'

Colonel Tremblay has something to offer, thankfully. 'The cocaine smuggled into Saint-Pierre comes from Newfoundland by way of Quebec or Ontario. This has been our experience.'

Relieved, plus I've had lots of time to think about this very point. 'Johnny Smith, as we all know, served time for just that crime. If he's back in business, isn't it possible that he's now connected with someone who's flown from Martinique to France and then to Saint-Pierre? We know that cocaine from South America is reaching Europe via the Caribbean. Why not divert a fraction of it to Saint-Pierre, smuggling it aboard the direct flight from Paris? French territory to French territory via France.

No customs checks.'

'That someone being Philippe Jean?' inserts Staff Sergeant Windermere—unnecessarily, but taking the opportunity to make her presence known.

'That's my theory.'

'That direct flight only runs in the summer,' Colonel Tremblay points out. 'The last one for this year was on the second of September.'

'I can confirm that Philippe Jean spent time on the Burin Peninsula in September. I suspect that following his arrival he toured around the peninsula, including, I'm willing to bet, a sidetrip to Lamaline, before returning to Saint-Pierre, and eventually flying back to Martinique via Montreal.'

There you are—another piece of the puzzle for your consideration.

Inspector Bowmore looks around the room following the translation session between the *gendarmes*. No one—*aucune personne*—among them has anything to add during the time it takes for what I said to to sink in?

Inspector Bowmore does. 'Didn't Philippe Jean suspect you might be onto him? Wouldn't he have done something to put a stop to your nosing around while you were in Martinique, while he had the chance?'

'Like kill me?' I'm tempted to smile. 'Philippe Jean was well aware that you all knew where I was and my reason for being there. If anything had happened to me he would have been suspect number one.'

'I don't mean kill you. I mean blackmail you. Do something, anything to shut you up.'

Back to the business of the photograph, which I have already set aside, which I'm not about to revisit.

'I'm not that easily intimidated. He might have had it in his mind but . . .'

'I have a question.' Colonel Tremblay interrupts, a curt disregard of French civility. He pauses. 'Does the name Céline mean anything to you?'

An abrupt, unforeseen smack between the eyes.

From which I recover, hopefully without detection. 'You mean the singer. Amazing voice. That performance from the Eiffel Tower . . .'

'I mean a Céline you met in Martinique.'

'Let me think.' Which I pretend to do.

'Let me be of help, Mr. Synard. According to the commanding officer of *la Gendarmerie nationale* in Fort-de-France, she worked at a bar on the beach in L'Anse à l'Âne, which we understand is the village where you stayed while in Martinique.'

'I see.' I'm hesitating, which does nothing but prolong the agony. 'It's possible. I did stop at a bar on the beach.'

'For a BAM. A beer, I understand.' He glances at Bowmore, then looks back at me. 'You might also be interested to know that the police in Martinique have an extensive file on this Céline. She has a reputation for photographing tourists in embarrassing positions. I think you call it "selfie." How would you say in English, "pornographic selfie?"'

He had considerable trouble pronouncing the last phrase. Regardless, he's expecting a response. Nothing from me other than additional sweat.

The surrounding faces are all mercilessly blank.

The colonel nods to Inspector Bowmore to take charge, a reflection I assume, of her greater command of English than his own.

'We've been informed that she used these selfies to blackmail her victims by threatening to send them to addresses she tells them she found on their phones after the victims passed out.'

The damn cops in Martinique—painstakingly thorough.

'In fact, that wouldn't work because even if the phone has Face ID, it won't unlock when the owner's eyes are closed. Some of her victims knew this and called her bluff, and a couple of them even had the courage to report her to the police. But others, whether they bought into her line or they were so hung-over they couldn't think straight, panicked and paid what she demanded.'

'I paid nothing to anyone named Céline.'

'But according to the police in Martinique, Philippe Jean did. For a certain photograph, one which I don't feel we need to describe, with which we assume you're familiar.'

I don't respond. My silence they take for a yes.

Frederick steps in. 'Sebastian, we all realize this is awkward for you. We assure you that this is a police matter that does not go beyond the confines of the various departments involved.'

'Thank you.' Some measure of relief. 'Thanks.' I hope the gratitude is showing through my chagrin.

The others try not to stare at me, but clearly the ball is in my court.

'I have no recollection of the picture being taken. My first knowledge of it was when it showed up in my companion's email.'

'Do you have any idea how it got there?' asks Inspector Bowmore. 'That we haven't been able to figure out.'

'As a matter of fact . . .'

A slight lift in my hapless self-esteem.

I turn to Colonel Tremblay. 'You'll recall Monique, the owner of the shop in Saint-Pierre, Impromptu, and the woman who set up the photo shoot with Zach Russell.' He nods. 'When Mae and I visited her shop, Mae gave Monique her business card.'

'So, she passed the contact information to Philippe Jean?'

'Yes, that's my conclusion. And I also know for a fact that Monique has visited Martinique several times over the past few years.'

The colonel's face is the most expressive it's been since I entered the room. He's veering toward agog but is not quite there. And following translation, so is Lieutenant Charpentier.

'Are you thinking, Mr. Synard, that Monique and Phillippe Jean had a partnership well before he showed up in Saint-Pierre?'

'Yes.'

'And are you thinking it may have involved more than his clothing design business?'

'It's possible, yes. Am I thinking cocaine? That remains to be investigated. Unfortunately, I don't have the resources to do it myself.'

I avoid pointing to the obvious—the *brigade de recherches* does. Observing Lieutentant Charpentier post-translation, it would seem I've set his brain cells in motion.

'Very good, Mr. Synard.' That's about as effusive as the colonel is likely to get.

The primary focus remains, of course, on who is responsible for the death of Zach Russell. The possibility of cocaine smuggling, and yes, thankfully, even the infamous photograph, are secondary to proving who drove a knife into the young man's thigh, hastening his death.

Inspector Bowmore continues, 'As we wind down I'll remind everyone that Johnny Smith is in custody awaiting arraignment for assaulting Sebastian. Of course we'll be working together to build the case against him for the murder of Zach Russell.' More for my benefit than theirs, I'm sure.

Adds Colonel Tremblay, 'An indictment would follow the relocation of the suspect to Saint-Pierre and Miquelon, the jurisdiction where the murder took place.'

And Staff Sergeant Windermere, 'Of course.'

'From your perspective, Sebastian, are there gaps that need to be filled if and when the case proceeds to trial?'

It's Frederick. He could be sincere. He could be giving me an opening to further redeem myself in the eyes of the other four.

I'm thinking maybe he is.

'I believe the key issue is Johnny Smith's attitude toward his brother. Was it reason enough to drive him to harm Zach Russell, the relation he believed was somehow responsible for Jody being gay? On a more basic level, does Johnny Smith think Jody had a choice? That if he and Zach Russell hadn't entered into a relationship Jody would somehow be straight for the rest of his life?'

Everyone sits in silence. At least two of them know what I'm saying is hitting me personally. That it's not just Jody I'm thinking about.

'At its core, is this a hate crime?'

No one answers.

'A hate crime that escalated to murder?'

I look at Frederick, acknowledging the question.

I have thought about this a great deal. I've tried to look at it from the perspective of a father.

'Intentionally? I don't know.'

I look about the room, in turn catching the wilfulness in each of them.

'But I hope for what you hope for—that in the end justice will be done.'

I walk away knowing my part in the drama has largely ended. Out of courtesy I will be kept updated, and if the case goes to trial I'll be called to testify.

Just as I reach my car in the parking lot I hear a version of my name, '*Sébastien*.'

I turn to find Colonel Tremblay waving to me. He catches up.

'*Guy*,' he says, stretching out his hand.

Suddenly we're on a first-name basis. I must have done something right inside the room.

'I want to thank you personally. You have helped to fit the pieces together.'

'No problem.'

'I admit at times I was doubtful.' He shrugs. '*Merci*. As you say in English, you live, you learn.'

'*Que será, será*.'

It throws him off. For some reason I always thought that was French. Apparently not.

'Can I be of help to *you*?' he asks.

'I'm not sure what you mean.'

'The photograph.' He pauses to let it register. 'I assure you it was not as *risqué* as some on her phone.'

Good to know, but not much consolation. I do the shrugging.

'Would it help you if I call your partner and explain about Céline?'

Straight out of the blue.

I'm suddenly considering a new path to redemption. One that I never would have thought of had it not been just handed to me. Handed to me by the commanding officer of *la gendarmerie*, the man at the centre of the investigation into the business of the "pornographic selfie." Now my friend, Guy Tremblay.

(I hear faintly the noise of crowds cheering Guy Lafleur and Mario Tremblay, as I did during the Montreal Canadiens' four-Stanley Cup dynasty of the 1970s.)

As I take a moment, not wanting to look too eager, the man adds, 'I can imagine she was upset.'

'Royally pissed.'

It looks like he's not so sure about the first half of the idiom. The second half is clear enough.

We both chuckle. It brings a boost, an upturn in morale.

It's a straight-on, man-to-man alliance. I'm not sure the French would understand a shoulder punch. I opt for a thumbs up, together with a punchy '*Très bien*.'

I'm uncertain what Mae's reaction will be. She could think I put him up to it. That we're in cahoots, although she's had enough experience with *la gendarmerie* to know they only play by the rules.

'I'll let her know to expect your call.' And at the same time make sure she understands it was the colonel's suggestion, not mine.

He's about to head back inside. We shake hands.

'Thank you. I appreciate this.' It's not the last we'll see of each other, I hope.

'*Bonne chance*.'

I'll need it.

ELEVEN

A LOT HAS happened since my encounter with the battery of police officers, mostly without direct involvement from me. Johnny Smith has taken up residence in a cell in Saint-Pierre, awaiting trial, sometime in the new year. Lieutenant Charpentier and his squad have dug deeper into the Monique–Philippe Jean connection and found it predates his arrival in SPM by at least two years. Not only that, but Monique appears to have been in the company of Joy Monplaisir enough to suggest something more than sharing fashion tips. And as for Amélie Dubois and boyfriend Théo, it looks like they have a choice of coming clean now or facing the consequences of what is sure to come out in the trial.

The courtroom will be crowded. There'll be a parade of witnesses, including the Caribbean swimwear designer/suspected drug dealer.

The parade will include myself, and Nick, who made it through the term with reasonably good marks considering all he went through. He arrived back in St. John's yesterday. I'm thankful and relieved to have him home again. Well, much more than that. I'm on cloud nine, somewhere I haven't been for a long time.

Or as pleased as punch, as I said (in vain) to the colonel when I called to thank him once again. '*Très content*,' I added. It did the trick.

As a consequence of his phone call to Mae, the two of us have reached an understanding. There will be no further mention of said photograph. We have resumed a romantic entanglement . . . I guess you could call it now. A relationship that's not what it was, as yet. It will take time. I'm willing to speed things up. She's not quite there yet.

Basically, we'll see how it goes. If I've learned anything, it's that there's nothing about Mae that I should take for granted.

As the colonel said, you live, you learn.

And as I said, you give it a try, you hope for the best.

Gaffer races to the front door from the kitchen, where I've been working on supper. The mutt's been anticipating Nick's return. It's been a couple of hours since he left the house for a beer at Bannerman Brewery. With a friend from university, I assumed.

Gaffer's yelping is not for Nick alone. It tells me there's a second person at the door. I turn the burner to simmer and exit the kitchen to check it out.

The fellow is unknown to Gaffer.

But not to me.

'You remember Jody,' Nick says haltingly.

'Of course.'

'I invited him for supper. You don't mind?'

'Absolutely not.'

What I expect now is an explanation. Yet I try not to look as if I do, given it would be totally awkward for them both. There's no way their encounter could have come about by accident.

'I'll hang up your jacket,' Nick tells him. 'Have a seat in the living room. How about I open a bottle of wine? Jody, you good with white?'

It could be just another day in the Synard household. A friend drops by; we sit back and shoot the breeze. Could be, but, plainly, not.

When the wine has been poured and the cheese and crackers passed around, the room is no less expectant. The time has come, the Walrus said.

'So, Dad, you must be wondering.'

A slight, disciplined nod.

I'm looking at Nick, but Jody is the one to go straight to the point.

He turns to me. 'I had no idea what to think when I got Nick's text. He wanted to meet. He said it would be good for both of us. I wasn't so sure. I mean we both lost the guy. That's what he said.'

As painful as it must have been, I can see Nick doing that. Just helping Jody work things through.

Nick knows what that's like. Getting past the divorce, for one. Which was far from easy, through no fault of his own.

'How did you get Jody's number?'

'Frederick.'

'I could have given it to you.'

'I wasn't sure you'd think it was such a good idea.'

He's probably right. At the least I would have raised a lot of questions.

Introspection wasn't something he was open to. By the sound of it his mind was already made up.

'It's been good for both of you?'

I gather it has, without either of them admitting it outright. Whatever they talked about they keep to themselves.

I can deal with that. The fact that Nick invited him for supper says enough. I guess. For now.

'Jody is staying in Torbay between semesters.'

'With Austin.'

'That's good.' He's found an alternative to going home.

'You're welcome to come by,' Nick tells him.

'As often as you like,' I say.

'Thanks.'

He looks at me more intently.

'I'm sorry about what happened. Johnny forced me into it.'

Nothing added.

Somehow it all seems staged. The smiles forced, as if we're each playing a role. With no more than a surface connection between me and either of them.

It continues through the curried chicken and wild rice. The meal is a diversion at least.

Jody will soon head back to Shiwak Hall. He needs study time, he says. He has one more exam to write. In a couple of days Austin will pick him up.

Still nothing about his brother.

'I'll walk back with you,' Nick tells him, moving to the closet to retrieve their jackets.

'It's been hell.' Out of nowhere, Jody's words cut the air.

Ardent, intently sombre.

'Fucking hell, actually.'

Nick is back, without the jackets. Jody looks at him.

'They think we're freaks. They think they got the right to tell us how to live. It's fucking hard when it's your own family.'

He starts to fill up.

I get to him before Nick. I wrap my arms around him. I can feel him shaking.

He doesn't break. He holds it together as he draws away.

'I'm okay. I'll walk back on my own.'

'You sure?'

He's already at the closet. He puts on his jacket, turning to Nick.

'Thanks for getting in touch.'

'No sweat. Maybe we'll see you again.'

'Thanks,' he tells me.

That's it. He's out the door, closing it behind him.

Nick and I are left standing there.

We turn to each other and hug each other for all we're worth.

ALSO IN THIS SERIES

One for the Rock
Two for the Tablelands
Three for Trinity
Four for Fogo Island
Five for Forteau